PROFIT MOTIVES

BRUCE DAVIS

Brick Cave Media
brickcavebooks.com

Profit and Loss

PAPERBACK ISBN: 978-1-938190-90-2

Printed in the United States of America.

Cover Illustration Artist: Ravven
Ravven.com

Brick Cave Media
brickcavebooks.com
2024

Dedication:

In memory of Weston Ochse, a brother in arms from different wars, but a brother nonetheless.
Until Valhalla, my friend.

Also by Bruce Davis

Available from Brick Cave Books

MAGIC LAW SERIES
Platinum Magic
Gold Magic
Silver Magic

THE PROFIT LOGS
GlowGems for Profit
Thieves Profit
Profit and Loss

PROFIT MOTIVES

BRUCE DAVIS

Brick Cave Media
brickcavebooks.com

Chapter 1

I was up to my elbows in tangled conduit, trying to trace an intermittent short, when Deuce stomped up the loading ramp and into the cargo bay. His face was grim and there was murder in his eye. Having seen that look before, I knew that anyone who got in his way would regret it - if they survived. I got carefully to my feet, but he didn't seem to notice me. He crossed the deck to the weapons locker without a glance in my direction.

"Everything Jake, Deuce?" I asked, keeping my tone casual.

He thumbed the lock, swung the locker's armored hatch open, and pulled out his pulse rifle. I crossed the deck toward him as he snapped a fresh power pack into the stock, then put two more in his pocket. He buckled on a web belt with a holster and four ammo pouches. His blackened steel Huang pneumatic went into the holster and he loaded spare magazines into the pouches.

"We going to war, Deuce?" I asked. Still, he didn't answer. "I should let Sylvia know if we need to button up the ship."

At the mention of her name, she chimed on my link, the tiny data node embedded in my right mastoid bone. "What's going on, Boss?"

"Not now, Sylvia," I said subvocally, the nanofibers in my larynx picking up the nerve impulses and converting them to speech.

Deuce didn't say anything, didn't seem to notice the slight pause as I communicated with Sylvia. He strapped a calf sheath to his leg and slid a long, narrow-bladed knife into it.

"Deuce, what's wrong?" I reached out and gripped his upper arm, dangerous given his present mood, but I was really concerned now. He glared at me for a second and then shrugged my hand off.

"It's personal, LT. Nothin' to do with you or the ship." He pulled out a small backpack and swung the locker closed, turned and stalked through the aft hatch toward his workshop.

I didn't try to stop him. Deuce stood just a couple of millimeters shy of two meters tall and was massively built; trying to stop him was like trying to stop a rockslide. He'd get where he wanted to go anyway, and you'd be on the deck wondering what hit you.

We were still at Highpoint for some resupply and repair time. It was a bit more expensive than other shipyards, but Cleo's killing on the Nucor stock deal meant we could afford it. Ten days before, we had finagled our way into the Kwai Hong complex on Ceres with the help of Sam Guthrie, a charter customer who'd taken a liking to us. We were there so Rabbit could slice an old database and learn the secret of natural glowgems.

The secret turned out to be more explosive than expected as Kwai Hong revealed to the system that natural glowgems were the larvae of the first extraterrestrial life form humanity had encountered so far. The revelation had tanked the glowgem market and Cleo had made us, and Sam, a lot of money, selling Nucor and other gem stocks short.

I had to admit, the shipyard here was better equipped than the one at our home base of Port Tycho on the Moon. For once, the *Profit* would get a full overhaul of her Moss drives and inertial dampers. Then we'd show the charter fleet what a fast interceptor could do.

I frowned at the idea of thinking like a charter boat captain. A year ago, I'd have wanted the extra speed to outrun the *Federales*. Now here I was being all respectable and businesslike. I sighed. Being a businessman opened doors and opportunities that would never have been possible back in my old freelancing days. It was nice to be respectable, all right. It was just so damn boring.

Deuce had spent the better part of the ten days since we'd returned from Ceres away from the ship. Just where, he hadn't said, and I hadn't wanted to pry. It was unusual, though. Deuce considered the *Profit* his only home and since his stepbrother Mike had been killed last year, he had no other family but the ship's crew – Cleo, Rabbit and me.

Deuce was the closest thing I had to a brother, and I'd be damned if he was going to blow me off when he was in trouble.

I followed him down the passageway, skirting the bulge of the reactor and drive unit. The hatch to Deuce's workshop appeared to my right. It was open and I could hear him rummaging through his locker. I paused at the hatch coaming and looked in.

Deuce's workshop doubled as his private quarters. It might be a combination machine shop and electronics junkyard, but it was also his home. The bulkhead next to his locker was hung with tools and instruments.

A workbench beneath the tool racks held a partially disassembled plasma injector and a riot of spare parts and components. In contrast to the chaos on the workbench, Deuce's bunk was tightly made with military precision. A broken hologram of Mike and Mike's wife, Mariko, taken on their wedding day, was carefully centered on a small shelf at the head of the bunk.

Deuce stood with his back to me. He pulled a shirt and light jacket out of the locker and stuffed them into his small backpack. The pulse rifle lay on his bunk, and he'd added a pair of throwing knives in wrist sheathes to his arsenal.

This was serious. The last time Deuce had armed himself to the teeth, we'd gone up against Colin Jones and his Red Dragon gang on their own turf. Jones was dead now, and the Dragons were too disorganized with infighting to make a serious run at us. So, who was Deuce planning to pick a fight with?

"What's going on, Deuce?" I asked.

He didn't look at me. "I told you it was nothin' to do with the ship, LT. It's my problem. I'll solve it."

"Sure you will, Deuce. But not solo. That's not how we do things on this ship."

"That's how it's gotta be this time." He sealed the backpack and tossed it on the bunk next to the pulse rifle. He finally turned to face me. His expression was flat and hard as moon rock. The only hint of his seething rage was the flushed skin that showed through the fine stubble of his scalp and the slight quiver of his blond beard as he ground his teeth.

I folded my arms and leaned against the hatch coaming. Deuce never talked much and whatever he'd been doing for the past few days was his business. If he wanted to tell me about it, he would in his own time. But this was different. He was arming for a war and if the last couple of days had anything to do with that, I figured it might be time for me to get nosy.

"What have you been up to the last few days?" I asked.

"That'd be my business, LT. And I'll thank you to get out of my way. I don't have a lot of time."

"Not until you tell me what's going on. You don't go to war on this ship without my say so. We're family here. Maybe not blood, but if someone takes on one of us, they take us all." A look of real pain crossed his face. I hardened my tone. "I'm not letting you leave here until you tell me what's going on with you."

He smiled grimly. "You think you can stop me, LT?"

"Don't try me, Deuce. We don't want to go down that road."

He glared at me for a second, then looked away, the pain returning to his face. "Aw, hell, LT. You know I couldn't raise a hand against you. Just let me go. I can't tell you why."

"Damn it, Deuce. Why can't you?" I took a step toward him, my hands low and open to show no threat. "When I was in the Bear, you never gave up on me. As soon as the war ended, you packed up and headed for Mars. You didn't even know if I was alive. And when Wu had me trussed up and was ready to turn me into his latest meat sculpture, it was you who pushed Cleo into coming after me. I can't let you do this alone. I owe you too much blood and sweat."

I moved closer; close enough for him to tag me if he wanted to. He just might if I pushed him too hard. Instead, he shook his head, and a shudder ran through him as if he were cold.

"They've got my daughter, LT," he cried. "I've got to get her back, but they'll kill her if I bring anyone else in on it."

I took a step back. Deuce had a daughter?

Chapter 2

A daughter? The idea of Deuce having a child seemed as unlikely as being able to breathe in a vacuum. I'd never known him to spend much time with women. Not that he didn't like them, but his liaisons tended to be one- or two-night affairs, usually with women he met in dives like the Blue Booby back in Port Tycho. It wasn't likely he'd know their real names, much less have a child with one of them.

"You never mentioned a daughter," I said.

Deuce shrugged. "Didn't know about her myself until ten days ago. Grace and me, that's her mother, Grace; we hadn't been in touch for a few years. I found Grace here on Highpoint when we got in a couple of weeks back, with the Guthrie charter."

I nodded. Sam Guthrie had said good-bye after our recent run to Ceres and I didn't expect to see him again soon. He was one of the richest men in the outer system, an ice merchant. He was also a former Marine squad leader. We'd bonded over mutual war stories, albeit on separate sides of the Reunification War.

"Grace and me didn't have a lot of time together. The ship left kind of sudden-like on the Ceres job, and I told her I'd be back for her."

We'd gotten back from Ceres ten days earlier. Deuce had obviously been with this "Grace" since we returned. I owed Sam Guthrie a big favor for his help on that job, although it had profited him as well as our own pockets. The news nets were still buzzing about the discovery that natural glowgems were the larvae of an alien life form. More muted was the information that synthetic gems were inert. The gem market had taken a hit, and Cleo had made us a lot of money selling gems stocks short. Sam had followed her advice and made his own killing, so maybe he wouldn't be calling his marker any time soon.

"When did Grace tell you about the girl?" I asked.

"The night we got back from Ceres. I went straight to the club where she sings and bribed the head waiter to give me a table right up front." He smiled. "I don't think she expected me to come back. She nearly choked up when she saw me. Had to restart her first number. I stayed after the club closed. We talked a lot. Don't really remember all what was said, but finally she told me about Ingrid."

"Ingrid," I repeated. "Is that the girl's name?"

Deuce nodded. "It was my mother's name. I told Grace about her once." He smiled again. "You should see her, LT. She looks just like my Ma when she was a little girl."

"You've seen her?" I asked, surprised. If this was a scam, it wasn't likely she'd risk introducing Deuce to the girl until later, after some money had changed hands.

"Yesterday, at breakfast. Grace has a nanny who watches Ingrid most nights."

I thought carefully about how to say what I needed to say next. "Don't take this the wrong way, Deuce," I said. "But you must have wondered, must have asked yourself..."

"Was she mine?" Deuce said.

I nodded.

"I admit to havin' my own doubtfuls at first," he said. "But Grace had the Birth Registration and the DNA print. She was born about nine months after I went to Mars to fetch you out of the Bear. She's mine, sure and certain."

Deuce picked up the backpack and unsealed it. He reached in and pulled out a small holoprojector. He held it in his open palm and pressed the base. The five-centimeter-tall projection showed a little girl with white-blond hair pulled back in pigtails. She wore a dark blue skirt and white shirt—some kind of school uniform by the look of it and looked out shyly from beneath long blond eyelashes. Her eyes were a deep blue, almost violet. Deuce's face softened as he looked at the image. She was a beautiful child, and I could see how she'd captivated him.

"When did they take her?" I asked.

Deuce's face grew dark again, and he turned off the projector. "This morning. She and the nanny were on the way home after shoppin' for a new dress, somethin' pretty to show off for me." His voice broke and his fists clenched as he said it.

"Easy Deuce," I said quietly. "We'll get her back." *Provided this 'Grace' person answers a few questions first,* I thought.

He shook his head. "They said I had to come alone, or they'd kill her." He held up a hand when I started to speak. "I ain't stupid, LT. I know it's the standard threat. But somethin' about the way the message was worded made me believe they'd know if I wasn't alone. And they'd do what they said without worrying overmuch about it."

"What exactly did the message say?"

"It was distorted, run through a voice print scrambler

so's it wouldn't be traceable. The voice said First Sergeant Sven Gulbrandsen should come alone and unarmed to a certain bar on deck 34 at 23:00 tonight or Ingrid would be found in a recycling bin with her throat cut. They were real specific about what they'd do to her. I got the impression they were military, or at least military trained. I gotta assume they're serious players, at least 'til Ingrid's safe. I can't risk bringin' you in, LT."

I nodded toward the pulse rifle on the bunk. "You're not exactly unarmed. I can see hiding the blades, maybe even the Huang. But where are you planning to hide the pulse rifle?"

"I ain't planning on walking into that bar on their terms, LT. I figure to get there a few hours early, do a little recon and tuck the rifle away somewhere. Maybe under a table or in the head. Then watch the traffic in and out for a while. I should be able to spot them before they see me. Whoever they send will have watchers. If I'm there first, I'll see how they set up their surveillance. Take out the watchers first, then take the messenger and make him tell me where they have Ingrid."

His plan was straight out of the Special Forces playbook and maybe tactically sound, for a four-man special operations team with good intel to back it up. Not workable for one man alone, no matter how capable. And if they had referred to Deuce by his real name and old rank, they'd probably read that playbook. Hell, they may have written it. I knew some of the old Black Ops commandos had escaped Mars and were operating in the Belt. Hans Metternich himself was out there somewhere, although my crew and I were the only ones who knew it for certain. Was that why they had made this run at Deuce? Maybe. Metternich would look for leverage wherever he could find it. Hook Deuce and he'd have to know I'd step in to help.

"Think it through, Deuce," I said. "You can't cover

all the angles alone. You might take one, even two, but they'll have enough coverage to drop you before you get them all, and then where will Ingrid be?" He stiffened as if to argue the point, but then his shoulders slumped, and he nodded.

"You need a team to make that kind of thing work," I went on. "And you can't be sure the messenger will know anything useful; probably won't if these guys are any good. Did they say anything else? Like what they wanted with you? Did they ask for any money?"

Deuce shook his head. "That's all. Don't make any sense to me. I don't have any money to speak of, and the Revolution and war were a long time ago. Hell, I was just a non-com. I didn't have access to anything really important. So, what do they want?"

"Any enemies I don't know about?" I asked.

He actually laughed at that. "You're better at makin' enemies than me, LT. At least the kind who'd do somethin' like this."

I had to agree with him on that. Deuce's enemies tended to be the kind who'd come straight at you. No screwing around with kidnapping little girls when a knife in the guts would do as well and be a lot more satisfying. But in our years together, I'd managed to piss off some seriously dangerous people, and my enemies were Deuce's by default. Kwai Hong had the juice to pull something like this off, but why? More likely he'd come at me directly, not through Deuce. And I couldn't see him teaming up with Metternich. Too much ego on both sides. The Dragons? Not likely. They hated Metternich as much as I did.

Chapter 3

"Who besides some of our old 'buddies' from the Black Ops group would know how to reach out to you?" I asked. We had encountered the remnants of the First Covert Operations Battalion a few years back, Black Ops commandos who had avoided capture after the war. The wild tales circulating through the nets of Revenants – Martian Way fanatics with a master plan to resurrect the Revolution – had a core of truth. And with Hans Metternich still alive to lead them, the tales weren't so wild.

"Nobody 'cept a few old NCO's from the Second. I'd trust any of them with my life. And Grace."

"Grace knows about your military background?"

Deuce nodded. "I got no secrets from Grace."

But she may be keeping secrets from you, I thought.

"Well, somebody who knows you from the old days is involved in this, and unless they want money, this is about leverage over you and maybe me as well."

"But, LT, I got no money to speak of. And they told me not to bring anybody else in. So how do you figure this has anything to do with you?"

I sighed in mild exasperation. "Deuce, you own a quarter share in this ship. We made a lot of money on the Ceres job, not to mention what's left from Jones' three-quarter million. You may not be rich, but you're not poor anymore either. Depending on the stock price of some of Cleo's investments, we could raise a couple hundred thousand on short notice." I paused to let that sink in. Deuce had never paid much attention to the money. Duty, honor, loyalty to his shipmates, and enough beer to drink, was the calculus by which he measured success.

"Does Grace know about the money we took from the Dragons?" A year earlier, we'd tricked Colin Jones into paying seven hundred fifty thousand yuan for a stolen cargo of embryos. Things went sideways in the exchange, and Jones had been killed by his own men, but we'd gotten away with the cash.

Deuce shook his head. "I never mentioned it. Truth is, I hardly think about it myself, except as it helped upgrade the ship. And Grace wouldn't talk about it if'n I had told her. She don't care about that kind of stuff."

"So if no one knows about the money, and Grace hasn't asked you for any, then the only reason someone would take Ingrid is to get leverage over you. And the only people who'd know your name and old rank are working for Colonel Metternich. That means it's a Third Directorate operation and that would involve me, too."

Deuce fingered the small holoprojector as he considered my words. His face darkened and he clenched it into his big fist. "The Colonel's not gonna leave us alone, is he, LT?"

"It doesn't look that way, Deuce."

His shoulders slumped and he nodded. "Okay, we'll do it your way. And you're right, I can't cover all the angles alone."

I reached up and grabbed his huge shoulder. "We'll get her back. She's your daughter and that makes her my family, too. We take care of our own."

Deuce nodded and put the holoprojector back in his pack. "We gonna tell Cleo and Conejo, too?"

"Yes, Cleo will skin me alive if I try to keep this from her. And we'll need Rabbit's help."

"Don't forget me," said Sylvia through the overhead speaker.

"Eavesdropping ain't polite," said Deuce with a slight smile. "Even for a computer."

"That hurts, Deuce. I may be an AI, but I'm family too."

"Where are Cleo and Rabbit, Sylvia?" I asked.

"Edward is in his cabin," she said primly. "And Cleo is not on the ship. Her link shows her to be on the Esplanade, near the Highpoint Bank and Trust." She was using her officious voice again, so I knew her feelings were hurt. I wondered for the thousandth time if it had been a good idea to let Rabbit program her with a female personality.

"Please get in touch with Cleo and ask her to come home as soon as possible." I looked at Deuce and pointed toward the hatch. "Deuce and I will be in the salon. Ask Rabbit to join us there."

"Yes, Boss," she said, still sounding sullen.

We crossed the cargo bay and climbed the ladder to the second deck. The salon was just aft of the landing at the top of the ladder. To our right was the catwalk that led across the open bay to the cockpit. To our left was the passageway to the living quarters and charter cabins. The salon opened directly onto the landing through a doublewide hatch. It was the largest and best-appointed space on the ship. The main common area was defined by a large sofa and three active contour chairs arranged around a low glass and metal table. Thick draperies and abstract tapestries covered the bulkheads, concealing their hull metal functionality. The dining area with a dining table and six chairs sat near the aft bulkhead and the hatch leading to the small but efficient galley.

A complex glass sculpture, a Diego Salazar original, hung above the sitting area. It had been a wedding gift from Rabbit. He never told me where he got it but had warned me not to try to get it appraised. I'd held on to it even after the divorce, in part because I liked it and in part because Cleo had wanted it. Now that we'd reconciled, we both saw it as a symbol of Rabbit's faith in us.

Rabbit was already in the salon when Deuce and I stepped through the hatch. He'd parked his powerchair by the dining table and had set up his virtual keyboard and holomatrix on the tabletop. He looked up as we entered.

Edward Conejo, alias Eddie the Rabbit, was a small man, thin faced with prominent upper teeth. His eyes were large and bulged slightly giving him a perpetually startled look. He'd been a data slicer for Martian Intelligence before the war and had been my cellmate in the Bear after being swept up in the first purges during the Revolution. He'd also been tortured in Metternich's biotanks. He had some of the genetic trait that allowed a bond with the nanofibers. He was paralyzed from the waist down as a result but could use his nanos to control his powerchair.

"Hi Zack. Hi Deuce," he said. "I didn't know you had a daughter. Wow, that's exciting! Sylvia told me all about it. We're going to get her back, right? I can help, you know. I've already sliced the security grid and have a search algorithm that we can tie into a facial recognition program. Then we can..." Rabbit babbled on in technogeek for a while. Deuce looked at me and shrugged in surrender. There had been bad blood between Deuce and Rabbit before last year's confrontation with Jones. Since then, they'd reached an understanding. Deuce still had little patience with Rabbit's frenetic speech and wandering attention span, but he respected his abilities as a slicer. Rabbit was the best in the business.

I let Rabbit run on for a while before holding up a hand to stop him. "That's great, Rabbit. But what we need now is to rig a tracker for Deuce. Something like the one you made for Cleo a few years ago so we can follow his link signal."

"No problem, Zack. I just need to record his base signal and then tweak the uplink function so it acts like a transponder."

"What if they don't take me with them?" asked Deuce. "What if this is just a meet and greet?"

"Like as not, it will be," I said. "They'll want to make sure you'll follow instructions. They may offer some proof they have Ingrid but probably won't tell you how to get her back."

"So, we tail 'em back to wherever they're based and get Ingrid back." Deuce's voice was flat, as if he were describing a walk across the deck. "We just have to be sure they don't slip the tail."

"That's no problem, either," said Rabbit. "Weren't you listening? I can track them with the security grid. If we can get a clear image of whoever Deuce meets, I can use a facial recognition program to follow them with images from the grid."

I nodded. "Get the tracker ready so we can follow Deuce in case they do take him to Ingrid. But we need a better way to follow them if they have a way to avoid the cameras. I managed to do it the last time we were here with a couple of bottles of fish sauce. We need to be able to follow them wherever they go."

Rabbit thought for a moment. "Give me an hour. I may be able to come up with something." He turned to the virtual keyboard and lines of code began crawling through the matrix in front of him. Deuce and I stood there for a few seconds, but Rabbit ignored us like we no longer existed.

Chapter 4

We left Rabbit to his work. It was only 18:00. We had plenty of time before the deadline. Plenty of time for Deuce to stew about it and get himself worked up all over again. I sent him back to his workshop. It wouldn't calm him down, but it was better than having him pacing the deck like a caged animal. I'd once seen a tiger in the New Pretoria Zoo pacing in front of the glass of its enclosure. All day long – back and forth. So much pacing that it had worn a groove in the concrete floor of its cage. I heard later that the tiger had turned on a keeper who brought it food, eating the hand that fed it. Deuce had the same look in his eyes as that tiger.

I watched Deuce slide down the ladder to the cargo bay, then spoke softly through my link. "Where's Cleo, Sylvia?"

"She's in a public tube capsule approaching the spaceport. She should be here in another ten minutes."

"I'll be in our cabin. Ask her to see me before she talks to Deuce."

“Yes, Boss,” said Sylvia. “Is there anything I can do to help?”

“Scan the local net. See what you can find out about this ‘Grace.’ She’s a singer, probably in one of those places on the Esplanade.”

A half second later, Sylvia answered, “There’s a Grace Tyler singing at the Planitia Club on the Esplanade and a Grace Lumumba at the Zero G on deck 13.”

Somehow, I didn’t see Deuce in a zero-g scrum ball. His Grace sounded like a higher-class girl than that.

“Run a background check on Grace Tyler. Don’t tell Deuce. Forward whatever you find to my link.”

“Do you think she’s running some sort of scam on Deuce?” Sylvia asked, a definite protective edge in her tone.

“I don’t know anything yet,” I said. “Just get me the information.”

“Will do, Zack.”

I walked aft to the cabin I shared with Cleo. It was a generous space for a ship the size of the *Profit*, nearly four meters by three, set dead aft on the second deck. Like in the salon, the bulkheads were hidden behind fabric, swaths of muted green and pastel blue. A double bed, covered with matching plush pillows and a thick duvet, was centered against the curving bulkhead opposite the hatch. A pair of matching chairs with thick green cushions flanked a round table in the center of the cabin. Cleo’s vanity, a compact rosewood table with an oval mirror, was to the right of the hatch. Bottles of perfume and cosmetics forming a phalanx of colored glass along the rear edge of the tabletop. My battered metal locker looked out of place along the bulkhead to the left, like a rotten tooth at the edge of a debutant’s smile.

I opened the locker, pulled out my old black fatigue pants and black pullover sweater and tossed them over one of the chairs. At the bottom of the locker was the lockbox where I kept my Huang pneumatic and a pair of throwing knives in drop sheathes. I knelt to thumb the lock and a dreadlock of hair drifted across my face. I brushed it back, suddenly irritated by it. I lifted the Huang in its worn clip-on holster. It slid smoothly out of the dark stained leather, feeling good in my hand.

I looked around at the cabin. Cleo's work: her sense of style and understated grace was all over it. I slid the Huang back into its holster and set it on the table next to my clothes. I kicked off my shoes and stripped off the work pants I was wearing before pulling the shirt over my head. My hair caught in the shirt's collar and tumbled across my forehead. I shook it back. The dreadlocks were Cleo's idea; I'd never like them.

I sighed and pulled on the black fatigue pants and clipped the Huang to the waistband. I crossed back to the locker and reached into the lockbox for the throwing knives. The hair swirled forward again. I frowned, pulled out the knives and slammed the locker. Enough playacting. Deuce was in trouble, and we were going to war again.

Shaving my head took less time than I'd expected. I rinsed the thin layer of shaving gel from my now smooth scalp and rubbed a hand over the chocolate brown skin. It felt good; like I had stripped away a year's worth of lethargy and was suddenly wide awake. I pulled the sweater on over my head and rolled up the sleeves to strap on the wrist sheathes.

Cleo swept into the cabin as I was rolling down my sleeves. She took in my outfit and my shaved head and frowned. I looked at her and felt the familiar pang of longing and lust that she always brought to me. Her skin was the color of Saigon cinnamon. Shoulder-length, straight black hair framed her heart-shaped face. Her body was small -

compact and powerful as a coiled spring. But it was her eyes that always arrested my attention. Almond shaped and emerald green with flecks of gold that seemed to swirl deep within them. They could take a man to ecstasy or despair with a single glance.

"You're looking grim," Cleo said as she shrugged off her short blue jacket and hung it on the back of her vanity chair. "What's the emergency? Sylvia just said you needed me home right away."

"Deuce is in trouble. Someone has taken his daughter and is using her as leverage to get at us."

Cleo hardly reacted to the words 'Deuce' and 'daughter' being used together. She pulled a slim brown cigarette from the silver case she kept in her purse, flicked it alight and inhaled the fragrant smoke. She breathed out slowly and said, "Tell me."

So, I told her - about Grace, about the little girl, about Deuce's rage and his plan to try to take the kidnappers alone. "I'm having Sylvia run a background check on this 'Grace Tyler'. Rabbit's working on a way to track both Deuce and whomever he meets at the bar. Deuce's plan is a good one for a team operation. I figure we can back him up and either track the messenger back to the main group or take out his handlers and force him to talk."

Cleo had moved to one of the armchairs in the middle of the cabin as I talked. She sat silently smoking for a while after I finished. She shook her head and snubbed out her cigarette in the ashtray that popped out of the arm of the chair.

"You're gearing up for a fight before you know for sure that this girl is really Deuce's daughter," she said. "Stop and think. We're not in the wild black beyond here. This is Highpoint. They have cops and security forces to deal with this sort of thing."

"You're right about one thing," I said. "This is Highpoint.

Graft and corruption are art forms here. I wouldn't trust the Highpoint cops to investigate a fart in a public men's room. Maybe if Akira Kensai was still alive, but he isn't. We'll take care of our own."

"We can't risk that, Zack. We're not a tramp freighter trying to scrape by from job to job with nothing to lose. We have a real business here. Think about how we've been treated this trip compared to the last time you docked at Highpoint. You can't tell me you don't like being welcomed and respected. We could lose everything by going off on some adventure to rescue this girl."

"This girl is Deuce's daughter."

She shrugged. "So you say. Do you know that for sure? Who is Grace Tyler and where has she been for the last six years?"

"I don't know," I said with more anger than I intended. "And I don't care. All that matters to me is that Deuce believes it and he needs our help. Now are you in or out?"

She held my eye for a second before looking away with an exasperated sigh. "I'm in," she said. "This is a family affair. I just wish you'd talk to me before you commit to something that puts us all at risk."

I stepped close and pulled her to her feet. She didn't resist. I put my arms around her, and she melted into me, returning my embrace.

"Deuce and I need you," I whispered into her ear. It wasn't just an endearment. Cleo was a formidable weapon, the best unarmed fighter I had ever seen. We needed her with us if we were going into a tight spot.

She looked up into my eyes and smiled. "Yes, you do. Someone has to do the thinking around here." She kissed me lightly on the lips. "Now go see Deuce and let me change clothes. I can't kick bad-guy butt in a skirt."

Chapter 5

We assembled in the salon an hour later. Deuce still had that caged animal look in his eye, but at least he'd stopped pacing. Rabbit sat at the table where Deuce and I had left him, still noodling on his keyboard and looking smug, though he actually looked up when Cleo entered.

Cleo was dressed for action in a one-piece form fitting jump suit and ankle length combat boots. She wore a narrow black belt with a slim needler holstered on her right hip. Her electrostatic stun batons were strapped diagonally across her back, jutting a little above her left shoulder where she could draw them easily. Strapped to her right ankle, she carried a combat knife with a twelve-centimeter double-edged blade.

Deuce smiled slightly at the sight of her and nodded his thanks. They exchanged a look that said more than words could convey, like two predators acknowledging one another's abilities.

"What have you got for us, Rabbit?" I asked.

He turned his chair to face me and handed me a

small disc. "That's the tracker for Deuce's link. Sync it to your own link and keep it in a pocket or on your belt. It'll flash a directional arrow in the heads-up display of your contact lens monitor, just like the one you used to track Cleo to Jones' safe house a few years ago. I improved the design so the tracker is smaller, and it will read out range and elevation as well. You can suppress the display with a double blink, just like the targeting system in the heads-up function." He turned to Deuce. "I've got something really *jiaohua* for you. Zack wanted a way for us to follow the person you contact, even if they get past the security net cameras. I checked the system, and there are some areas of the station that aren't well covered by image monitoring. Mostly automated levels and 'bot maintenance yards, closed to human traffic but not inaccessible. Of course, if they'd followed my advice three years ago, they'd have tighter security and people like me wouldn't be able to slice their system." He paused for a second, as if realizing he was getting off course. He had gotten better at that over the past year. Living on the ship, dealing with clients, interacting with Cleo and me, had changed him.

"Anyway," Rabbit continued. "I thought about what substances would stand out and be detectable with the station's internal sensors. You know, what could we mark a target with that would be detectable no matter where the target went?"

"Get to the point," Deuce interrupted.

"Oh, sure, Deuce," Rabbit stammered before reaching into a pouch slung from the arm of his powerchair. He handed Deuce a small square of what looked like shiny paper.

"What's this?"

"Inside the foil is a gel tab. It'll adhere to most smooth surfaces and will soak right into cloth, like a soap bubble.

It contains a trace of Zylene HD."

"Drive coolant?" I asked.

"Sure," Rabbit said with a triumphant smile. "I realized there were coolant conduits everywhere. The gravity grids are just variants of Moss drive technology. I found out there are leak detection sensors in the maintenance grid. They're extremely sensitive but aren't keyed to the alarms like radiation sensors are. I can use them to trace even this tiny amount of coolant wherever Deuce's contact goes. Deuce just has to get close enough to tag him with it."

Deuce held up the small square of foil. "How's it work?"

"Peel the top layer off, palm it with the foil side toward your hand and touch him anywhere with it."

"What if he's the careful type and don't let me get close enough to touch him?"

Rabbit shrugged. "I don't know. Throw it at him? You just need to get a gram or so of the stuff on him somewhere."

Deuce started to speak, but I held up a hand and interrupted. "This won't get the attention of the cops, will it?"

"No," Rabbit said. "The sensors are only keyed to routine maintenance alerts. Someone may send a 'bot out if the target stays in one place too long, but once we know where they're keeping the girl, that won't be a problem."

I nodded. "Good work, Rabbit. I want you and Sylvia to monitor things from here. We're heading out early to do a little recon around the meeting site."

Rabbit looked disappointed. Maybe he thought he should come, too. He was mobile enough in his tricked-out chair, but conspicuous. Not that any of us could easily blend into the crowd on Highpoint. In Port Tycho, a trio like us, armed to the teeth, wouldn't draw a second look. Here we'd stand out like whores at a prayer meeting.

Rabbit was more valuable monitoring us from the ship and steering us around official notice.

"I need you here, Rabbit," I said quietly. "You're into the official net. We may need you to do some fancy slicing if the local law decides to interfere. "

He grinned at that. "Let them try."

We made our way to Deck 34 with a minimum of notice from the locals. Rabbit steered us around crowds and, at one point, opened a secure hatch so we could access a maintenance dropshaft that took us down the last fifteen decks.

On Highpoint, status and class determined where one lived. The arcology was a huge cylinder, thirty kilometers long and almost six in diameter. The outer shell was two hundred meters thick and housed all the life support, reactors, utilities and service personnel that allowed the elite class to live in the tall fairy towers and manicured parklands of the open central core. Bars in the lower decks catered to the working class.

The bar on Deck 34 didn't have a name, just a cheap holosign saying "BAR" that glowed in the air above a doublewide hatch off a dirty, nondescript passageway. The traditional swinging saloon doors sagged, and one was propped open with a length of cargo strapping. The passageway had once been a small commercial center, but the bar and a pawn stall were the only open businesses. Several empty storefronts, three-sided three by four-meter spaces with the fourth wall open to the passageway, faced the bar. The passageway followed the gentle curve of the arcology's hull to the left and the right. We were deep enough that there was no attempt to straighten the curves like they did on the upper decks.

Deuce entered the bar, and Cleo followed a minute later. I set up in an empty storefront diagonally across from the place. Deuce pulled out his shirttail to cover the

Huang in its belt holster and carried the pulse rifle rolled in a leather jacket. Cleo wore a white quilted jacket that concealed her batons and needler. The knife at her ankle was black and blended with the color of her boots. It was hardly noticeable unless you looked. Besides, she had other assets that drew the eye away from her feet. It was 21:30, ninety minutes before the scheduled meet.

The storefront must have been a restaurant or food stall at some point. A thin sheen of grease covered the floor and walls. The air in the depths of the stall still smelled faintly of fried fish. I knelt in a dark corner, out of sight from the main passageway, but with a full view of the bar and the passage to the left, the antispin direction. The arcology turned on a twenty-four-hour cycle to simulate day and night on the open central core. Directions around the circumference were designated "spinward" or "antispin" based on the turn of the station.

"I'm in position," I said subvocally over my link. "Deuce, Cleo, what's happening in there?"

Cleo answered. "I wish you'd speak out loud. That trick you do with your nanos make you sound like a cheap AI with a stutter." Her voice was barely audible above the noise in the background. "Deuce is set up at the back of the bar. Other than a couple of lewd propositions, I haven't seen or heard anything unusual. No sign of a surveillance team."

"Good," I said. "We got here first. Can you see the spinward corridor?"

"I've got a good view from the front of the bar."

"Stay sharp, and don't let Deuce drink too much beer."

"He's not drinking at all from what I can see," she said.

That was unusual. Even on a job, Deuce liked his beer. His capacity was prodigious, but he never let it get the better of him.

I settled in to wait. I figured Ingrid's kidnappers would

scope out the bar about an hour before the scheduled meeting, set up their surveillance inside and outside, possibly even in this very stall, and then call in their messenger.

Ten minutes passed, then twenty. They'd be coming any minute. I eased a kink in my left calf and touched the Huang on my hip for the twelfth time. The big man appeared as a shadow at the edge of the stall's open side, easing out of the darkness along the spinward wall. He was backlit by the dim light in the passageway and was facing me, his face concealed by the darkness.

He stepped into the opening, and I revised my impression of his size. Deuce was big. This guy was a giant. His head seemed to touch the overhead, and his shoulders were wide enough to take up an appreciable fraction of the opening. He had no visible neck or waist. His legs looked thicker than the *Profit's* landing struts and were just a shade shorter.

He stood on the threshold, sniffing the air like a dog, swiveling his huge head back and forth. My hand went almost involuntarily to my Huang and my nanos tingled. He moved fast for a big man. Even with the nanofibers speeding my reaction time, he managed to get a hand on me. The Huang cleared the holster as I dodged aside. If I'd been a millisecond slower, his big hand would have locked on my throat. Fortunately, his left hand only grabbed my right shoulder. Unfortunately, he had a grip like a mechanical claw. Pain shot through the joint, climbing up my neck like steel spiders and shooting electric shocks down my arm. The Huang clattered to the deck. His thick arm straightened and lifted me off my feet, driving me back into the rear wall. I grabbed his wrist with my left hand. I felt the nanos augmenting my strength, and I twisted his wrist with everything I had. I might as well have tried to twist a titanium rod.

He drew his face close to mine. His breath was hot and smelled of harsh tobacco and cheap vodka. He grunted and pulled a small flash from his pocket. He shone it into my face. It cast enough light for my nano augmented eyes to see his face as well.

It was Earth Asian, not Chinese but broader and flatter with rounder looking eyes. It was a face that had been hit a lot, enough that it knew there was nothing to fear in being hit and his eyes showed it. I've known brave men who were called fearless, but that's not what they were. They'd mastered their fears and pushed through them to do what had to be done. This was a man who truly knew no fear. His eyes were completely indifferent to the prospect.

"She's in there, yes?" His voice was a breathy whisper. His vocal cords had been damaged sometime in the past and had never recovered. He spoke with an accent, and it was clear that English wasn't his first language.

"Who?" I managed to gasp. The pain was subsiding but only because I had lost all feeling below my shoulder.

He shook me casually, like a cat shaking a bit of yarn. "You know who. The pretty little girl. The one they took away."

"No, she's not," I said. "We're here to meet the people who took her."

"Why? Don't lie, I smell lies just like I smell you hiding in here."

"She's my partner's daughter."

He shook me until I thought my arm would tear off. "You aren't old enough to partner with her *baba*. I told you I smell your lies."

"No, *shi hua,*" I gasped. "They took her yesterday. We're supposed to meet them at the bar at 23:00."

He gave me a token shake, but his eyes crinkled up at the edges, as if he were in pain. Maybe thinking hurt him.

It struck me as funny, given that he was doing a good job inflicting pain on me. I must have smiled.

"You think me funny?" he rasped.

"No, I just think you've got the wrong guy. Or the wrong girl. If you didn't take her, then I've got no cause to hurt you."

He smiled at the thought of me hurting him. But he eased his grip and let me slide to the floor. He didn't turn me loose, but the grip was now merely tight, not painful. I looked at my right hand and tried to wiggle my fingers. Maybe they moved a couple of millimeters.

"She's not here?" he asked, somehow making it sound like a threat. Maybe it was the fist the size of a soccer ball that he held above my head that made it seem that way.

"No, man. We're trying to get a lead on the guys who took her so we can get her back."

I'm not sure he heard me. His eyes seemed to glaze a bit. "I've been looking so long. Eight years. Since Antarctica. I saw her up on fancy shopping plaza outside spaceport, but she got in drop shaft and went down before I reach her." He spoke as if he were talking to himself, reminding himself of what had happened, so he'd be sure to get it right. His eyes snapped back to me. "Maybe you not lying. I must be mistaken."

He let go of my arm and straightened my jacket. He picked up the Huang between a thumb and forefinger and looked at it as if it amused him. He handed it back to me. I still couldn't move my right arm, so I took it in my left hand, upside down, by the grip. He turned and walked away. I thought for a second about trying to turn the gun around and point it at him. Tell him to freeze and tell me what the hell he was talking about. But I didn't. I shook all over and was glad to see him disappear into the shadows to spinward.

Chapter 6

“Zack,” Rabbit’s voice over my link was high pitched with alarm. “Who was that? I saw him go into the stall but can’t see the interior. Are you alright?”

“Still breathing, Rabbit,” I said. My arm was moving again, at least below my elbow. Moving my shoulder didn’t seem like a good idea just yet. “Did you get a shot of his face?”

“No, it was too dark. Geez, he’s big. Bigger than Deuce, even. What did he want?”

I thought about that for a whole second. “I’m not sure. At first, I thought he was talking about Ingrid, but that wasn’t it. Maybe he’s just a crazy jolthead, his brains burned out by the drug so he doesn’t know what year it is, much less who he’s talking to.” But as I said it, I knew it wasn’t so. If his brain was addled, it wasn’t from drugs, or even the cheap liquor on his breath. “See if Sylvia can tail him through the security net. A guy that big shouldn’t be too hard to spot.”

I transferred the Huang to my right hand and found

I could hold it. Maybe even point and shoot it, as long as accuracy didn't count. I tried not to think about what the big man's hand could have done to my throat. I prodded my shoulder and winced, but the pain was subsiding. The bones felt intact under my probing fingers. I blocked the pain fibers with my nanos and found I could move the shoulder reasonably well.

Cleo chimed in on my link. "Showtime," she said. "I've got three men coming down the spinward passageway."

I knelt again, the Huang now steady in my hand. The nanos in my optic nerves activated and my vision shifted into infrared. I could see the three as they advanced past my hiding place. One of them stopped and motioned the other two forward. He drew a long-barreled Steinbauer needler and looked left and right, up and down the passageway. Then he backed into the opening, watching his partners but not looking behind into the dark where I crouched. I eased the Huang's safety off. It was well oiled and made no sound.

The man stopped a couple of paces in front of me and knelt. I raised the Huang but thought better of it. A pneumatic isn't loud, but it isn't silent either. For a second, I wished I'd brought a needler with sleeper darts, but then thought better of that, too. We wanted to avoid trouble and tail these guys back to Ingrid, if possible. I waited in the dark, my augmented senses watching for any sign that this guy realized he wasn't alone.

My link chimed, the sound loud in my ear but not audible to the man in front of me. "This is it," Cleo said. "There's one guy checking out the bar and another heading toward Deuce. They haven't made me yet. Where's the third one, Zack?"

"About a meter in front of my nose," I answered subvocally. "Watching the bar."

"Are you still good?"

"Golden. He's looking the wrong way. How's Deuce?"

"The meeting is going down now. The second guy still hasn't made me."

I kept the Huang out, ready. The guy in front of me had settled into an easy ready position. He wore a dark, close-fitting shirt and fatigue pants. He held the Steinbauer in a two-hand grip, low and rock steady. No fidgeting, no wasted motion. He carried himself like a professional.

He cocked his head as if listening, then said a few words in a low murmur. Even with the nanos boosting my hearing, I couldn't make them out. His tone was calm, almost bored. The meeting in the bar was going as planned.

As if in confirmation, Cleo's voice came through the link. "Deuce is talking to the messenger now. I can't see the guy's face, but Deuce looks calm enough."

The man in front of me spoke into his link again. He lowered the Steinbauer and took a few cautious steps forward, peering toward the bar. I tightened my grip on the pneumatic.

"They're moving, Zack," Cleo said. "I think Deuce managed to mark his man. He grabbed the other guy's shoulder when he went to stand up and said something to him. The guy left the bar in a hurry and his buddy left a few seconds later. I'm going to follow them."

"Hold your position," I said. "The guy with me isn't moving." Cleo would understand. It was sound tactics to leave a man behind to check for a tail. He'd wait a few minutes before leaving, just to make sure Deuce had followed instructions and had come alone.

Rabbit's voice replaced Cleo's on my link. "Deuce marked him, Zack. We're picking up traces of the coolant as he moves along. Sylvia and I will be able to track him."

I didn't reply. The man in front of me was watching the bar, focused and ready. I kept the pneumatic trained on his center of mass, the best point to aim in low light. A head shot would put him down before he could sound any alarm to his buddies, but if I missed, I might not get a second shot. Center of mass may not silence him as surely, but I was unlikely to miss.

"They're gone," said Cleo. "Deuce is still sitting at the table. How long do we wait?"

"Five minutes," I subvocalized to her.

Four and a half minutes later, the guy in front of me muttered something into his link. He stood and relaxed his two-handed grip on the needler and rolled his shoulders as if working out a kink in his muscles. He half turned as he started to replace the Steinbauer in its holster. He froze. Something had caught his attention, maybe a gleam of reflected light or a small sound or some other subliminal signal that told him he was not alone. He spun toward me, sweeping the needler up in a tight arc to cover the corner where I crouched.

I fired twice. The pneumatic made flat spitting sounds, about as loud as a rock dropped from shoulder height onto a concrete deck. The needler never fired. The man in front of me doubled over at the waist as if struck by a hard blow. He exhaled loudly as the pneumatic rounds punched into his abdomen and fragmented, just like they were designed to do. Deadly to flesh and blood, but not likely to punch through a pressure hull and kill everyone inside with explosive decompression.

He staggered forward a couple of ragged steps before collapsing at my feet. "Shit," I said as I lowered the Huang. "Cleo," I spoke clearly for the link this time. There was no one nearby to hear me. "Are you still in the bar?"

"Yes," she answered. "Is your man gone?"

"In a manner of speaking," I said. "Rabbit's got a good track on the messenger. Deuce tagged him all right. We'll give them a few more minutes head start and then follow."

There was no need to discuss the shooting just yet, or to mention the big guy who'd almost ripped my arm off. I'd fill her in on that later.

I bent down and went through the dead man's gear and pockets. His clothes were heavy military issue fatigues, black synthetic nanocloth pants and shirt, and heavier web belt and shoulder sling. The belt held a holster for the needler and two spare magazines, a pouch with a transit pass for the shuttle to Alta Hesperion, and a sheath with a military grade fifteen-centimeter-long combat knife. His pockets were empty, no ID, no spare change, no personal items. He had a cross belt slung over his left shoulder and clipped to the belt, as if he planned to carry some heavier weapon, but it was empty. Just a couple of clips on the front where a heavy pulse rifle or grenade launcher would hang. I'd seen similar rigs in the Special Forces when operating against ground targets. Carrying a grenade launcher aboard a space station was foolish. So what was he planning to carry with the cross belt?

I inspected his hands last. No Dragon tattoo on the left palm, but there was a small black teardrop on his left wrist, just below the base of the thumb.

"Double shit," I said. I wasn't surprised. This guy was a Black Ops commando, from the First Covert Operations Battalion, Metternich's Own. That meant Ingrid's kidnappers were very bad people, indeed. And that I had been right: this wasn't about money. It was about Colonel Metternich. And me.

"Deuce, Cleo," I said. "Out front now." I dragged the dead commando into the dark corner and left him there. I didn't know how long it would be before he was missed, but we wanted to be elsewhere if someone came looking for him.

I met Cleo in front of the bar, and Deuce joined us

a second later. He'd taken the wrap off the pulse rifle. The jacket was draped across his broad shoulders and he held the rifle at low ready. His eyes were hard and his face drawn and grim.

"The bastard gave me a picture film of Ingrid with a time stamp from early this morning on it," he said. "I almost tore his head off right there in the bar. Conejo better be able to track that *baotu.*"

"Rabbit has a good trace. He'll be able to track them," I said. "We have a bit of a problem, though. The lookout they posted in the storefront with me is dead. If he has some sort of a check in routine, they'll be on to us sooner than we want."

"You had to kill him?" Cleo said. "Couldn't you have taken him alive? He might have told us where they have the girl."

"Not possible. He was three meters away with a needler pointed at me. I was just faster." I paused and she nodded. "Besides, he would have been hard to break, at least in a time frame that would do us any good. He has a black teardrop tattoo on his wrist."

Deuce swore softly. Cleo's eyes widened. "They're back?" she said, only half questioning. "Why now?"

I shrugged. "I don't know." It had been a year since Metternich was supposed to have died a second time on the Moon. The *Federales* may have known he was still alive, but they weren't letting on. As far as the official story went, Recker killed him on the Moon and Kwai Chang Wu dumped the body in space somewhere between Port Tycho and Kwai Hong One. No DNA to check, nothing but the confession of a Martian loyalist that he altered identity records to establish the Middleton alias the Colonel was using.

"They took Ingrid to draw Deuce and me out," I went on. "The Colonel knows us both well. He knows I'd back

Deuce up, no matter what. He wants leverage to force us to work for him, but on what or why, I can't guess. He tried to recruit me back on the Moon, when we were sitting on those stolen embryos. I turned him down, but he's never been one to take no for an answer."

"So let's go get Ingrid before they know we're coming," Deuce said. "Then we can tell Metternich to take his Revolution and stick it where the sun don't shine."

"What did the guy you met in the bar say to you, after he gave you the image film?" I asked.

"He said this meeting was a test, to see if I would follow instructions. Then he gave me the picture and said they'd be in touch with more orders. That's when I grabbed his shoulder."

"Anything else?"

Deuce shook his head. "No, just that they'd be in touch with more orders."

"Anything odd about him? Is there anything he didn't say that he should have?"

Deuce screwed up his face, remembering the exchange. "I don't know, LT. He sure didn't seem too scared when I grabbed him. I figured it was because he knew he had back up. But he didn't make any threats about hurting Ingrid. And he didn't warn me off trying to follow him."

A thought struck me. How heavy was a six-year-old? Ten kilos? Twenty? Easy weight to carry in a sling hung from a cross belt. We couldn't follow the messenger back to his base, because they had no base, at least not on Highpoint. They were staying on the move, drugging Ingrid or intimidating her into silence so they could carry her from place to place until they made contact with Deuce.

"Rabbit," I said urgently through my link. "Where's our target?"

"Three decks up and about four frames spinward of your position. It looks like he's making for the tube stations on Deck 31. I got a pretty good look at his face as he exited the bar. I can use it to track him in the tubes. All the capsules have security imaging."

"Don't bother," I said. "He's heading for the spaceport. Find me the fastest route to the departure area from here. Put it in my heads-up display."

Deuce was already moving to spinward. Rabbit didn't answer, but a half second later, a map popped up in the lower corner of my visual field. At least Deuce was headed in the right direction. Cleo and I hurried to catch him. We ran half a kilometer until the arrow on the map made a right-angle turn. I pointed to the right, following it, and we found a service lift. The doors opened as we approached and slid shut right after we entered. Rabbit had sliced the lift AI and was in control. We shot up thirty-two decks in two and a half seconds and tumbled out into a crowded commercial corridor.

The arrow in my heads-up display pointed to the right and we took off at a dead run. Any thought of blending with the crowd was forgotten. People dodged out of our way and several pointed hand recorders in our direction as we passed. We'd be all over the social nets in ten seconds and the police nets two seconds after that. Highpoint cops were touchy about citizens carrying weapons in public areas, especially in the high-priced shopping zones that fed their protection racket.

Rabbit led us up a couple of moving stairways and down a broad concourse toward the spaceport. Up two decks and another half kilometer straight ahead. We passed the tube station on the left.

"Where's our man, Rabbit?" I called.

"He's in the cargo port, almost to the main berthing area."

I veered right at the passenger terminal and ran toward the cargo port. Rabbit flashed our berth number to the AI controlling the gate and it ignored us as we ran past. If it noticed our weapons, it didn't show any sign of it. I hoped Rabbit had disabled its alarms as well.

"Where is he, Rabbit?" I called as we reached the long row of docking bays that comprised the main cargo port.

"Bay 62, far end of the port. Hurry, Zack. They have a launch clearance and they're getting ready to depressurize the bay."

We pounded down the long concourse, Deuce racing out in front, Cleo just at my heels. The huge doors of Bay 62 were closed. Deuce banged on the door controls, but they were locked, the red outgassing light turning slowly above the center seam.

"Rabbit," I said. "Override the door control."

"I can't. They've already opened the outer door. They're launching."

Deuce stepped back and fired the pulse rifle at the door, screaming in incoherent rage. He held the trigger down, sending bolt after bolt into the doors. The packets of coherent microwaves hissed and crackled as they dissipated into the station's hull.

"Deuce, stand down," I shouted.

He stopped firing and looked at me. He shouted once and sent one last bolt into the door, then lowered the pulse rifle, breathing hard.

"Where are they headed, Rabbit," I asked.

"They filed a flight plan for Alta Hesperion," he answered. "They're just leaving the Highpoint zone of control now." He paused a second. "Aw, shit, Zack. They went dark. They disengaged their transponder as soon as they entered freefall space and engaged their drive. There's no way to tell where they're going."

Chapter 7

Deuce was pacing again. He'd slung the pulse rifle on his back and pounded his fists against the sealed doors until his knuckles bled. Cleo finally got him to stop and held him by the shoulders as she spoke quietly to him. I didn't hear what she said, but it seemed to calm his rage. He was now merely agitated instead of berserk.

Ten minutes later the red flashing light above the doors' header turned green and the doors hissed open. Deuce charged through the opening into the empty docking bay. There was nothing to see. The bay had the clean-scrubbed appearance it gets after all the loose debris has been flushed out into space. No telltale bits of plastic or incriminating notes. No juicy clues dropped by clever captives. No scrawled messages hastily written on the inner airlock doors. Those things were for realie dramas. In real life, bad guys often made clean getaways. Especially well-trained, well-funded bad guys.

"Deuce," I said quietly as he searched the bay. "There's nothing here. Anything loose was blown out into space when they outgassed the bay."

He stopped, his face a mask of pain and helplessness.

"I let them get away, LT." His voice was soft, almost a whisper. His empty hands hung at his sides, fingers open, no longer clenched in rage.

"There's nothing more we can do here," Cleo said, touching his limp hand. "If they meant to harm Ingrid, they wouldn't have gone to the trouble of setting up the meeting. They'll be in touch."

He nodded, allowed Cleo to take his hand, and we started out of the bay. We got as far as the doors before a short man in a stylish business suit met us. His skin was deep black. Not the dark chocolate color of my own, but an ebony black that spoke of either Earth origin or expensive genetic augmentation. He was shorter than Cleo, probably no more than 160 centimeters, but lean and wiry. He stood casually in the open bay doors, arms folded across his chest. He didn't flinch or step back as Deuce and I towered over him.

He ignored me and looked Deuce in the eye. "Mr. Gulbrandsen, my name is Gabriel Zameda. I think you and I need to have a conversation."

Deuce said nothing. I stepped closer and said, "I think you need to piss off. Deuce and I are returning to our ship."

He swiveled his head to look at me. His eyes were dark, almost black. He smiled slightly, a flash of white between his thick lips. "I'm a Federal Agent, Mr. Mbele. Your friend is a person of interest in a federal investigation."

"You're mistaking me for someone who gives a damn." I started to elbow him out of the way. I stopped when I heard the whine of a pulse rifle powering up. Two men in black utility fatigues stepped into view from the concourse, weapons leveled at me.

"And you're mistaking this for a request," Zameda said.

Deuce took a step to the left and came up on the balls of his feet. One of Zameda's men shifted his stance to cover him. I made a hand sign to Deuce, and he stood down.

I smiled at Zameda. "Always happy to cooperate with the government."

He smiled, too, but the smile didn't reach his eyes. No one was fooling anyone here. He gestured to his men, and they lowered their pulse rifles.

"After you." He stood aside and extended a hand toward the concourse.

We walked back the way we had come, past the bay where the *Profit* waited for us, and out to the main terminal. Zameda directed us to the right, into the administration complex. There was the usual security scan and they made us check our weapons, which didn't sit well with Deuce. They gave us receipts, all nice and legal, which was supposed to make it all right. It didn't, but the phalanx of armed guards around the security scanner made it hard to protest.

They separated us, of course. It was standard procedure. Deuce was led away first, down a narrow corridor and into a room on the right. Cleo and I were placed in our own rooms and told to wait. The doors were locked as soon as our escorts left, so waiting was about the only thing I could do. The room was about three by four meters, clean but not sterile, well-lit by glowpanels overhead. There was a metal table and three chairs, two on one side of the table and one on the other. Two for the people asking questions, one for the person answering them. I tried to open my link, knowing it likely wouldn't work. Blocking comms was a standard Fed procedure, too. With nothing else to do, I sat in one of the paired chairs, facing the solitary one. I leaned back, put my feet up on the table and settled in to wait.

After about thirty minutes, the door opened and Zameda walked in. He glanced at me, at my feet, and at the single chair across the table from me. He frowned for a brief second before pulling out the chair. He looked at my feet again, then flicked some imaginary dust off the sleeve of his expensive jacket and sat down. He set his datapad on the table, lining the bottom edge up precisely with the edge of the tabletop. He sat back, looking relaxed, but said nothing. He shifted his eyes slowly and pointedly to my feet, then looked back at me.

I sighed and swung my feet to the floor. “Happy?” I asked.

He took a small, folded leather wallet out of his breast pocket and opened it, laying it on the tabletop for my inspection. It was real leather, well made and expensive looking. Inside was a hologram of his face and DNA print and the name Gabriel Zameda in black lettering. Under his name were the words “Special Agent in Charge.” Opposite his picture, on the other side of the fold, was a holographic badge with gold script spelling out the letters F.B.S.

Zameda tapped the badge. “I’m Special Agent Gabriel Zameda,” he said, as if I couldn’t read that for myself. “You don’t have to talk to me. You aren’t under lawful detention and there are no recording devices in this room. I’d like to ask you some questions about your activities today.”

I said nothing.

He folded the little wallet and put it back in his breast pocket. It didn’t make a bulge. Nor did the sidearm that I was sure he carried. It was a very expensive suit, probably custom made. I wondered how a *Federale*, even a ‘Special Agent in Charge,’ could afford a custom suit.

“I’ve already spoken to your partner, Mr. Gulbrandsen. And to Ms. Lee.”

I said nothing.

“The three of you were carrying quite an arsenal. Nothing illegal, but an unusual assortment of arms for the crew of an expensive charter operation.”

I said nothing.

“You don’t talk much, do you?”

“Oh, was there a question in there?” I asked.

I saw a flash of anger in his eyes, but he quickly controlled it. He smiled that professional smile that interrogators use to put you at ease. I flashed it back at him.

“Why were you chasing that man down the concourse?” he asked.

“Were we?”

"Security imaging shows you hurrying down the concourse to Bay 62." He spun the datapad around. It lit up with an image of Deuce, Cleo and me running down the concourse, obviously taken from an overhead security camera. He went on, "You got to the bay a few seconds behind the last person to board the ship in that bay. You tried to open the doors. Mr. Gulbrandsen even fired a pulse rifle at them. So, who were you chasing?"

"An acquaintance. He owes Deuce a debt."

"You need that much firepower to collect a debt?"

I shrugged. "We're cautious. You never know what class of people you might meet in a strange place."

He smiled at that. This time the smile did make it to his eyes. He was genuinely amused. He picked up the datapad and flipped through several screens. Then he replaced it on the table, turned so I could see it.

"Do you know this woman?" he asked, indicating the image in the pad's matrix.

It was a professionally produced image, a publicity shot or a portfolio picture, of a striking woman with platinum blond hair. She was dressed in an expensive looking evening gown, cut to flatter her slim lines and slight figure. Her eyes were deep blue, almost purple and she wore an amethyst pendant that hung low on her neck. The color of the stone matched her eyes.

"Never saw her before," I said. Which was true, although I knew who she was. I hadn't exactly lied, but I hadn't answered his question either. Zameda may have been careful to present this as an informal conversation, but intentionally lying to a *Federale* could open a world of problems that we didn't need right now.

He shook his head. "That's not what I asked. Do you know who she is?"

I had to give him some grudging respect. He may have been an overdressed prick, but he was a smart overdressed prick.

"From Deuce's description of her, I imagine that's Grace Tyler."

"She and Mr. Gulbrandsen seem to be quite close. Were you aware of their relationship?" I didn't like Zameda's sly tone but kept my face neutral.

"None of my business who Deuce spends time with."

"Did you know they lived together for several months seven years ago?" Zameda asked with a barely concealed smirk.

"I was in Brunault prison seven years ago. I didn't know if I'd live or die on any given day. Who Deuce was shacked up with wasn't a big concern of mine." I wasn't giving this smug asshole a millimeter.

He tapped the datapad. Grace's picture was replaced with an image of Ingrid, the same one Deuce had in his little holoprojector. "Grace Tyler has a daughter, a six-year-old. She's about the right age for Mr. Gulbrandsen to be her father. Has he told you if he has a daughter?"

"Why don't you ask him? Or ask Grace Tyler who the father is. Why should you care?" Again, I was careful to avoid an outright lie.

"I did ask Mr. Gulbrandsen. He's refused to answer any questions at all. He hasn't said a word beyond confirming his name since we brought the three of you in here."

I laughed. Name, rank, ID number. That's all they'd ever get out of Deuce. "If Deuce doesn't want to tell you about the girl, then it's not my job to enlighten you. And if we're not lawfully detained, then we don't have to answer any questions at all."

He nodded. "That's right. And I have no intention of detaining you, but the girl hasn't been seen in a day and a half and there are rumors that she's been kidnapped. That would make it a Federal matter, especially if she's been moved off this station."

"How do you know she's missing?" I asked. "Has her mother reported it?"

He smiled that professional interrogator's smile again. "No. We have regular, if loose, surveillance on Ms. Tyler. She's usually quite attentive as a mother. The girl hasn't been seen in almost thirty-six hours, however, which is unusual."

I felt a cold sensation in the pit of my stomach. "Why are the *Federales* watching Grace?"

"Oh, we keep an eye on all former operatives from the Third Directorate," he said in an offhand way. Then his tone became more pointed. "Even you and Mr. Gulbrandsen."

He stood, picked up the data pad and tucked it under his arm. "You and your crew are free to go," he said. "I may have more questions for you, so please let us know if you decide to leave Highpoint."

"Is that an order?" I asked.

He smiled one last time. "Not yet. Call it a suggestion."

Chapter 8

We presented our receipts to the desk sergeant at the security station, and he gave us back our weapons. He didn't look too happy about it but, as Zameda had said, we weren't carrying anything illegal. He had no choice.

I looked pointedly at Deuce as he stowed his pneumatic and his knives. He looked defiant but said nothing. We'd have words once we got back to the *Profit.* Cleo looked thoughtful as she picked up her batons and needler. She slid her knife into its ankle sheath and walked toward the exit without a backward glance at the desk sergeant, or at Deuce and me. I sighed. There would be a lot of words once we got back to the ship.

Deuce and I walked together in silence with Cleo five paces ahead. We got to our own berth in a few minutes, and Cleo entered our registration number to open the airlock doors. Deuce and I had caught up to her by the time the doors opened. Cleo started across the open bay toward the ship. I made to follow, but Deuce stopped me with a hand on my arm.

"I ain't going back to the ship, LT," he said. "Grace will need me, and we've got to figure out where they took Ingrid so's I can get her back."

I started to say something, but Cleo beat me to it. She must have overheard Deuce because she spun on her heel and stalked back to him.

"Don't you dare try to pull that crap now, Deuce Gulbrandsen." She poked a finger into his chest. "Do you know what Zameda threatened to do? He threatened to freeze all our accounts. He can do it, too. All he needs is a hint that we're concealing a federal crime. And guess what? We are. We need to turn over everything we have on Grace and Ingrid and do it soon or we'll be stuck in limbo until he decides to let us go. So, you're staying put until we figure a way out of this shit."

"That's why I have to leave the ship," Deuce said. "This is my problem. I got to be the one to solve it."

"It's too late for that," Cleo shouted. "We're already involved. Zameda suspects there's information missing from the official record about those stolen embryos last year. If he finds out about the money we took from Colin Jones, we'll be labeled as accessories, and they'll seize all our assets."

"They can't prove anything about the money," I said. "Hank Boucher is the only one close enough to that case to suspect anything and he wouldn't give us up." Hank was a cop in Tycho City, a former guard from the Bear and a friend. He'd saved my life more than once in prison and had testified against Metternich and his cronies in the war crimes trials that had followed Reunification. We'd built a friendship of sorts based on an uneasy combination of shared experience and shared respect.

Cleo groaned with exasperation. "They don't have to prove anything. They can freeze the money and the assets while they complete an investigation."

My respect for Zameda jumped up to a new level. He'd played it perfectly, hitting each of us where we were vulnerable. He knew Deuce would never talk, so he did all the talking. About how much trouble Deuce was causing for his shipmates, no doubt. He'd threatened Cleo with a racketeering investigation. Just the sort of drawn out, shadowy case that could drag on for months or years and bankrupt us, destroying the financial security she'd worked so hard to build. For me, he'd used the fact that Deuce hadn't told me about Grace's background to try to drive a wedge between us. And it was working. At least to the extent that I was seriously pissed off at Deuce and agreed with Cleo. This wasn't the time to break ranks.

"Cleo's right, Deuce," I said. "We need to stick together."

Cleo didn't grab Deuce by the ear and drag him back to the ship. She used his collar. But from where I stood, the effect was the same. He went without protest.

We climbed the ladder to the starboard sally port. I hadn't given a lockdown code when we left, so the port opened immediately.

Sylvia began scolding us immediately as well. "Where have you been? Edward tracked you into the administrative section, then we lost you. He couldn't access the security systems in the Federal installation. They're on a separate system from the regular Highpoint grid. I've been worried sick about you."

"You're an AI, you can't get sick," I said.

I opened the weapons locker and Deuce stripped the power pack from his pulse rifle, passing it to me. Cleo leaned in and stowed her batons.

"Don't make jokes, Zack. Where were you?"

"We were having a pleasant conversation with a Federal agent." I finished stowing the weapons and sealed the locker as Deuce and Cleo started for the ladder. "What did you find out about Grace Tyler?"

"You can ask her yourself," Sylvia said frostily. "She's in the salon with Edward."

Deuce stopped in his tracks. "Grace is here?"

"I just said so," Sylvia replied. "She called looking for you. Edward spoke with her and decided she should come straight here rather than try to find you." She shifted to a private connection to my link alone. "I wasn't in favor of the idea, Zack. I don't like what I found in the database."

"What did you find?" I asked subvocally.

"Grace Tyler is listed as a singer with the Planitia Club, but her wages are paid by a company called Tharsis Talent Management. It doesn't have a local office and there are no other employees of record. Then there's her ID file in the security database. She doesn't have any entry more than six years old, not even a birth certificate or citizenship record. It's like she didn't exist before that. And there are file references that I can't open – higher security encryption than even Edward has been able to slice." She paused. Her voice took on a conspiratorial tone. "He thinks they're Martian Third Directorate protocols."

This was no longer news, but it did confirm what Zameda had told me. It was both disturbing and comforting. Disturbing because of what it implied about Grace, her background, and who she was actually working for. Comforting because it meant I had been right about the motives behind the so-called kidnapping. I had been getting fat and complacent, losing my edge, as the day-to-day security of a successful business became normal and comfortable. At least I hadn't lost it completely.

"Thanks, Sylvia," I said. "What about the big guy who almost busted up our surveillance? Were you able to track him?"

"He went up six decks and into a pod flop about three frames spinward of the tube stations. Places like that don't have registers or security cams. We lost him there."

Pod flops were hotels of a sort. They rented sleeping pods, two-and-a-half meter long tubes that were stacked five high in rotating racks. Basic accommodations for poor people, or people who just wanted to sleep cheap. Cash up front, no ID needed. How that Asian giant could squeeze himself into a standard sleeping pod was beyond me. Maybe they had oversized units for visiting gorillas.

Deuce was already halfway across the hold, heading for the ladder to the upper deck. Cleo and I hurried to catch up. Rabbit met us at the hatch to the salon. Deuce brushed past him and rushed in. Cleo paused at the hatch coaming, watching Deuce. I looked at Rabbit, who shrugged.

"I thought it was better to have her here," Rabbit said. "Where we can keep an eye on her. Sylvia doesn't like her."

I smiled. Sylvia didn't like most women. "I got that impression. And I think you were right about Ms. Tyler. The feds as much as told me she worked for Metternich during the war."

Rabbit turned and looked at where Deuce was holding a small woman in a tight embrace. "Are you gonna tell Deuce?"

"I think he already knows."

Cleo glared at me. "Of course he knows. What I want to know is why he didn't tell us."

I stepped into the salon. Cleo followed just behind my right shoulder. Rabbit rolled in on the left. We must have looked pretty grim because Deuce turned to face us, his arm tightening around the woman's shoulders.

Grace Tyler was smaller than I had expected. The image Zameda had shown me hadn't given me any clue to her height. She was almost as tall as Rabbit would be if he could stand. The top of her head barely reached Deuce's chest. Still, she faced us, standing as straight and as tall as possible. Her eyes were even more striking in person, wide and deep - dark midnight blue. They seemed unfocused, as if looking at something far away. I realized with a slight shock that she was blind. Deuce hadn't mentioned that, but then, he hadn't said a lot of things. Thinking about that made my anger flair again.

Deuce must have noticed because he spoke first. "Grace is with me, LT. Say what you gotta say, but she stays with me."

"You weren't straight with me, Deuce," I said. As I spoke, Grace turned more squarely in my direction and her eyes seemed to lock onto a point near the center of my chest. "Did you know Grace worked for Colonel Metternich when you were living with her?"

Deuce stuck out his chin. "Grace and me got no secrets from each other. I knew."

"Didn't you think that bit of information was worth sharing before we went after the kidnappers?" asked Cleo. I gave her a hard look, but she didn't take the hint. "We were willing to risk everything to help you get Ingrid back and you kept key information from us. If Metternich's people have taken your daughter, the stakes could be a lot higher than we realized."

"And if'n I'd told you, what then?" Deuce shifted his eyes from me to Cleo and back again. "Would you still have backed me?" He addressed me directly. "I didn't ask for your help, LT. I wanted to take care of this alone."

"And I stand by what I said. If somebody takes on one of us, they have to take us all. But you should have told me the whole story."

Deuce tried to stare me down but looked away after a couple of seconds. He knew I was right. "Didn't seem important right then," he said. "Savin' Ingrid was all that mattered. Anyway, Grace quit Metternich a long time ago. Back before the war ended. That's why we stayed out in the Belt. She ain't had nothing to do with the Directorate since then."

"Is that true, Ms. Tyler?" Cleo asked. She said 'Ms. Tyler' like she knew it was a lie and she was daring Grace to deny it.

Grace opened her mouth to speak but closed it again and half turned under Deuce's arm so she could look up into his face. "Sven," she said. "I'm sorry."

"For what?" Deuce asked.

Instead of answering she disengaged herself from his arm and took a step forward, facing us. She seemed to be looking into Cleo's face, except that her eyes tracked a little off center, toward Cleo's left shoulder. Still, it was uncanny the way she seemed to be able to tell where we were and who was speaking.

"You're Cleopatra Lee," she said. A statement, not a question. "Sven has told me about you. And you're right to question me. You don't know me and have no reason to trust me." Deuce stepped up beside her again, and she paused to intercept the hand he placed on her shoulder and squeeze it gently. Deuce didn't keep his arm around her, but stood close to her, hands at his sides.

She focused back on Cleo. "I, on the other hand, have every reason to be truthful with you. I need Deuce's help and, as Captain Mbele has said, that means I must enlist all of you.

"So, yes, I worked for the Third Directorate for a time during the Revolution and was on Ceres during the war as an operative for them. I never met Colonel Metternich in person, but knew he kept tabs on me. The directorate paid for the neural implants." She fingered the gem she wore around her neck. "And this pendant. They let me see through sonar transmitted to my visual cortex. Not detailed, but enough to find my way. And to 'see' people who are in range. My mission on Ceres was to try to compromise Kwai Chang Wu. I failed. Wu had no interest in me or in any other woman that I ever saw. During my time on Ceres, I heard stories about what was happening back on Mars. About the purges and the Death Squads and people disappearing into Brunault prison and never coming out. I didn't believe them at first. But then I met Sven, and he confirmed my fears and suspicions about the people I was working for. By the time we left Ceres, I had already sent the Directorate a letter of resignation."

Deuce interrupted her. "See, I told you so," he said.

I gave a harsh laugh. "You don't resign from the Third Directorate, lady. At least not while you still draw breath."

She nodded. "I know that now. I thought I could hide in the Belt with Sven. When the war ended, I thought the nightmare was over." She looked my way now. Her eyes seemed to find mine. "Then came word that Brunault had been liberated. Sven packed a bag and headed for Mars. I didn't understand at the time, but he asked me to wait for him, and I decided that I would."

"And yet you didn't," said Cleo. Her tone was harsh, accusatory. She stood with her hands resting on her belt, the right one near the needler. I figured she wouldn't shoot a blind woman in cold blood, but I wasn't a hundred percent sure.

Grace nodded again and a small shudder ran through her. She reached for Deuce's hand, and he took it, his meaty fingers caressing hers. She smiled, but it looked wistful, almost sad.

"No, I didn't," she said. Her tone was even, soft, and resigned. She clearly regretted leaving Deuce but wasn't intimidated by Cleo, either. "A few days after Sven left for Mars, I found out I was pregnant with Ingrid. I was angry and hurt that Sven seemed to care more about his friend than me. I was frightened. I didn't know anyone on Delilah and conditions there were primitive compared to the life

I'd become accustomed to. So, I ran away. I managed to bribe a freighter captain to take me to Alta Hesperion. I scraped by, singing for tips, until the Reunification Decree opened Mars to travel again. I slipped back into my old life in Planitia. Ingrid was born and I got a job keeping the books for a salvage company that was cleaning up war wreckage. Things seemed safe, if dull. And I was busy raising a small child."

She stopped again. A look of pain tinged with panic crossed her face and she struggled to control herself. "When Ingrid was three, they found me. I came home from work one day to find a man in my flat playing a child's card game with Ingrid. The woman I paid to watch her while I worked was dead, her body stuffed in a closet, although I didn't know that until later. He showed me the black teardrop on his wrist and gave me a simple choice – work for them or watch him cut my daughters throat before he killed me. We left with him for Highpoint that night." She turned to Deuce and placed her hands on his chest, looking up into his face. "I'm so sorry, Sven. I should have told you."

Deuce shook his head and wrapped his arms around her, holding her close. "It don't matter," he said softly. "I found you again. That's all that matters." He looked over the top of her head at me. "I'm standing by Grace, LT. Either on this ship, or off it."

Chapter 9

"Damn it, Deuce, that's not helping here. I can't afford to lose you." I turned to Cleo. "And you stand down. I'm still Captain of this boat. I decide who stays or goes."

Grace stepped forward and walked directly up to Cleo. If I didn't know better, I'd have sworn she could really see. She stood close to Cleo, not so close as to be a threat but close enough to get into Cleo's space and show she wasn't frightened. They faced each other for a heartbeat before Cleo surprised me by taking a half step back.

"You can stay here as long as you're with Deuce," Cleo said evenly. No threat or anger, just a statement.

"Thank you, Ms. Lee." Grace nodded her head slightly. "I know you've got no reason to trust me, but I swear I'll never do anything to intentionally hurt Sven or anyone else on this ship."

"Trust is earned. Right now, you're here because Deuce trusts you. Whether or not I do isn't part of that deal. Deuce is family, so no one here will make you leave, if he wants you to stay."

I looked from one woman to the other, feeling like there was some unspoken communication going on that I didn't understand. They stood stiffly, Cleo staring at Grace, and Grace standing very still, her unfocused eyes directed toward Cleo's face. Then suddenly the tension broke. Whatever message was sent had been received and understood. Cleo's shoulders relaxed and Grace turned slowly away and rejoined Deuce.

"What are we going to do about Zameda?" Cleo turned away from Grace and focused on me.

"Nothing right now," I said. "If he had any real information, he wouldn't be threatening us. He'd have frozen the accounts already and we'd be negotiating with him to get them back. The only real concern is that he'll get enough evidence to open a federal kidnapping investigation."

"Which is what we should give him right now."

"NO!" Deuce and Grace spoke at the same time.

Cleo wheeled to face Deuce once again. "Think, Deuce. They've taken Ingrid off the station. We can't track them. We need the *Federales*. We don't have the resources to do this alone."

"Well, maybe; or maybe not," Rabbit wheeled his chair into the salon. "We may be able to track them at least."

"You said they turned off their transponder," I said. "How do we track them?"

He smiled in that smug way he does when he knows something no one else knows. I frowned at him, and he stopped.

"Even without the transponder, they show up on the traffic control sensors – radar, lidar, gravimetrics. It doesn't matter if they run dark, someone knows where they are. The problem is picking one ship out of a couple of hundred on the sensor array, and then tracking it when it leaves the zone of control."

I nodded. "But you've come up with a way to do it, or you wouldn't be so damn smug."

Rabbit's smile returned. "Not me. It was Sylvia. She managed to get a good reading on their drive signature just before they shut down their transponder. I sliced the Highpoint traffic control data for her, and she tracked them outbound. Their flight plan was filed for Alta Hesperion and their initial plot was on track for that, but the acceleration was wrong. They'd overshoot and have to come back retrograde to dock there. It's possible to do it that way but stupid – too much time and wear on the drives. Better to slide downhill antegrade and match orbits with the station, then maneuver in to dock." He paused and looked around to make sure he had everyone's attention. Rabbit loved showing off, and he was in his element. "But if you wanted to make it look like you were headed for Alta Hesperion, when your real destination was the Moon, then the acceleration profile is perfect. Sylvia tracked them for long enough to nail down their best course for time and drive use. They're headed for the Moon."

That wasn't what I would have expected. Mars maybe, the Belt more likely, given that Metternich's current base of operations was supposed to be there. But the Moon? If they had tried to pick ground that gave me the advantage, they couldn't have done a better job. Which made me suspicious. There must be something I was missing.

"Where exactly on the Moon are they going?"

Rabbit looked at me and shook his head. "No way to tell unless we slice Lunar traffic control when they get close enough. Could be Port Tycho, Tranquility, or Gagarin Center or half a dozen smaller cities with spaceports."

"Can you slice them from here?"

He shrugged. "Maybe, but not easily. Too much lag. I can try, but I doubt I'll get very far."

I thought for a moment. Even if he could do it, the ship wouldn't be in range of Lunar control for another few hours and wouldn't commit to an approach pattern until just before landing. We had some time.

"No, never mind, Rabbit. It won't help us right now, anyway. At least we know roughly where they're heading."

"They'll go to Tycho City," Grace said.

Cleo turned to face Grace and Deuce once more. "How do you know that?"

The suspicion in Cleo's voice was acid, but Grace hardly flinched. "I overheard my 'manager' reserving a suite of rooms at the Dai Ichi, on the Promenade. I didn't think much of it at the time since I'm supposed to sing there next month. Now, I wonder why he'd make the reservation so far in advance."

The way she said the word 'manager,' laced with contempt and bitterness, caught my attention. Whoever this guy was, he'd be wise not to turn his back on her, especially if there were any weapons within reach.

"Who is this manager?"

"He calls himself Damian. A pompous name for a pig, and not his real one, I'm sure. His job is to make sure I do what they tell me. Mostly he puts his clammy paws all over me and threatens to hurt Ingrid if I resist." She paused at Deuce's sharp intake of breath behind her. She turned to him. "It's all right, Sven. You didn't know and I'm a big girl. I did what had to be done to keep Ingrid safe."

Deuce looked away. "But she ain't safe now. Not since I came back."

Grace thumped him on the chest, not in anger but not softly either. "We've been over that, Sven. I need you and Ingrid needs you. That's why I'm here."

"What do you mean 'that's why you're here'?" Cleo sounded less hostile, more concerned and curious.

"They contacted me two hours ago and told me Deuce had done what they told him to do. I'm supposed to sing at a private party tonight, at the Planitia. They said someone would meet me there with further instructions."

Cleo gave her a look that should have stuck at least four inches out of her back. I'd been the recipient of that look myself, so I knew it well. Grace, being blind, was immune, but she must have heard the change in Cleo's voice. "A little convenient, isn't it? Just as we're chasing down one of Ingrid's alleged kidnappers, they're calling you to set up another meeting. Has your daughter really been taken? Or are you part of this scam?"

Deuce's scalp flushed red, and he stepped in front of Grace. His voice was low but could have frozen methane. "You'll be taking that back, or we'll be having a problem."

Grace and I spoke at the same time.

"Deuce, stand down!"

"Sven, no!"

Grace was quicker. She maneuvered around Deuce's bulk and stood between him and Cleo. She shoved him back with both hands on his chest and then turned to face Cleo. She stood her ground. Her weird blind eyes that seemed to see everything held Cleo motionless.

"All right, yes, I worked for Martian Intelligence during the War. I quit. I had a baby. All I wanted was to live a quiet life and raise my daughter. But, like Captain Mbele pointed out, you don't just quit the Third Directorate. So, for two and a half years I did what I was told. I prostituted myself to that pig, Damian, swallowed what shreds of pride I had left and did whatever I needed to do to keep Ingrid safe. They left her alone as long as I played their game." She drew herself up and crossed her arms. She looked defiant, and fiercely angry. "And it worked. We had a life, of sorts, and Ingrid never knew she was in danger. Then you people showed up and everything changed.

I'm not proud of what I did, but it isn't my fault that my daughter is a bargaining chip in whatever game Captain Mbele is playing with the Third Directorate."

Cleo rocked back a pace as if slapped. She cocked her head as if seeing Grace for the first time. "I apologize. That was out of line."

She looked at Deuce. He didn't say anything until Grace prodded him in the ribs. He grunted and nodded once.

"Fighting each other isn't going to help Ingrid." I spoke quietly, but everyone looked at me as if I'd just appeared out of the black. "Grace, what can you tell us about this party at the Planitia Club?"

"Not very much. It's a private affair for some businesspeople from Ulan Bator. The Highpoint Trust Bank rented the club for the whole evening. The band and I are supposed to do our usual sets."

"Sylvia, is there anything on the nets about a private party at the Planitia tonight?"

"Searching," she said in the flat tone she used when her processor was accessing data. Then her voice shifted to the bright female personality that was her normal conversational tone. "I'll say there's something. It's apparently a big to-do for a high-level trade delegation from UB. The whole upper crust of Highpoint society will be there. Formal dress, invitation only, high security to keep the unwashed far, far away; all the trappings of serious money doing insider deals."

I turned to Rabbit. "Can you slice us an invite?"

He shrugged. "Hard to tell. I'll see what I can do, but it might be easier to slip in as hired help. I can slice us some catering credentials and background clearances, no sweat. Walking in the front door may depend on personal connections. Those are a lot tougher to fake."

Grace said, "The manager's not taking on extra help,

just making everyone work extra shifts. He's worried about temps screwing something up and making him look bad."

"Do you know any waiters or cook staff who owe you a favor?" I asked.

She frowned and shook her head. "My position there is a bit uncomfortable. I think Damian, or the people he works for, leaned on the owners to get me the job. Word about that gets around and nobody trusts you anymore."

"Rabbit, can you get me a guest list?"

"Sure, but what good will that do?"

"Just a hunch. See if Sam Guthrie's on it."

He opened his virtual keyboard, and his fingers danced in the air as he entered the search parameters. He grinned at me. "How did you know?"

"Like I said, just a hunch. But if you were running this shindig and found out that one of the biggest ice merchants in the system was in town, wouldn't you invite him? Especially since he supplies most of the water used here."

Cleo was shaking her head.

"What?" I asked.

"You're not going to try to beg an invitation from Sam Guthrie."

"Why not?"

She folded her arms and put on a face that implied I was a child or an idiot, maybe both. "Because we've abused his trust enough. He's an important client and we stand to lose a lot of repeat business if we piss him off."

"Sam likes me," I smiled back at her. "He won't mind. Besides, he made a lot of money selling gem stocks short. On your advice, I might add. I think he's sweet on you."

Cleo made a sour face. "That doesn't mean we can call him for favors. It isn't good business."

"If Metternich and his guys get their hooks into us,

we won't have a business for long. I don't know what he wants, and I don't like the fact that Zameda started sniffing around us just as a bunch of Black Ops commandos snatched Ingrid. There's no such thing as coincidence. This Damian character leaned on the Planitia's owner to get Grace a gig at the same time that we'd be here. We were set up, and I think Zameda knows something about it."

Cleo cocked her head at me, considering the connection. "You think he's working with Metternich?"

"Maybe. Or maybe he's working another angle and wants to use us to get to Metternich. Either way, we're in the middle. We need more information, and the only lead we have is this meeting at the Planitia. I want to be there when they approach Grace."

She thought about it for a few seconds more before nodding. I could tell she still didn't like the idea, but she didn't have a better one, except calling the *Federales*, and the rest of us had already vetoed that. Cleo could be stubborn, but she could also be persuaded.

"Sylvia, get me Sam Guthrie on the comm, please. Use the private locus he gave us."

"Yes, Boss."

A few seconds later, Guthrie was on my link. "I didn't expect to hear from you so soon, Zack. What's up? Has Cleo got another hot stock tip?"

"Hello, Sam. No, nothing like that. Actually, I'm calling for a favor. Were you planning on attending a reception at the Planitia Club tonight?"

He made a rude noise. "Only because Victoria isn't letting me get out of it. Damn silliness, if you ask me - getting dressed up in a tailcoat and lace to meet a bunch of politicians. I know the real power behind the UB mission and he ain't here. We've already done a deal that'll... Well, never mind that. It's not public knowledge yet. Anyway, what's that got to do with you?"

"Any chance you could get Cleo and me in?"

"The invitation is for 'Samuel Guthrie and party,' no mention of numbers. But why would you want to get in there? Has Cleo got some insider information I should know about?"

I laughed. Sam was a good drinking companion, but he was first and foremost a businessman. He'd gotten rich in a cutthroat market and never stopped looking for an advantage. "No. It's a personal matter. Best you don't know too much about it in case things go sideways. We'll try to stay out of your way once we're inside."

He didn't speak for a second. I was afraid I'd made a mistake in asking him until he said, "Now I'm really intrigued. I should tell you, the security will be exceptionally tight. Don't even try to get a weapon in there."

"It won't come to that." *I hope.* "Just a meeting with some people who have business with us."

"The kind of business that I might need to deny any knowledge of?" he asked.

"That's one way to put it."

"All of a sudden, this party sounds like it might be fun after all. It's a formal reception – tails and lace. They won't let you in wearing coveralls and boots. Can you dress the part? If not, I know a good tailor on the Esplanade who loans party dress to visiting businessmen."

For once I was glad that Cleo had insisted on upgrading my wardrobe as well as the ship. I had a set of formal wear, maybe a year or two out of fashion but serviceable, that she'd made me buy at a secondhand shop down in Freetown. I cleaned up pretty well, if the occasion demanded it.

"Thanks, Sam, but I'll manage. Where should we meet you?"

"At the Club entrance, around 19:30. It'll be better if I don't give Vicki too much time to think about you joining us. She won't be happy but won't make a scene in front of the fashion police who always turn out for this sort of affair."

I held my tongue. The current Mrs. Guthrie was twenty years younger than Sam and, from what I could see, excelled at two things: looking beautiful and spending her husband's money, not necessarily in that order.

"Until 19:30, then. Thanks Sam."

"Don't mention it. Maybe your business will liven things up a bit. Besides, I'd rather drink with you and Cleo than a bunch of fops with more fashion sense than business sense."

Chapter 10

I adjusted the cuffs of my tailcoat as the tube capsule slowed to a stop at the Esplanade station. I'd sprung for a private capsule and a ground transport to take us to the club. If we were going to look the part of high rollers, it wouldn't do to arrive on foot like common folk.

My tailcoat was rich navy-blue wool with black satin piping around the collar and tails. I wore matching wool pants with satin piping down the outer seams and my formal boots were calf length leather, soft as silk, and polished to a high sheen. The lace at my throat and down my shirtfront was pure white, less frilly than current fashion demanded, but classic in an understated way. The clothes fit me well and even though I felt more comfortable in tactical gear, dressing up occasionally felt good, especially with Cleo on my arm. I didn't have the lace cuffs peaking from below my sleeves that seemed to be *de rigeur* this season, but that couldn't be helped. I hated anything that might interfere with my hands anyway.

Cleo wore a floor-length, high-necked red *cheongsam* embroidered with a black lotus pattern. It fit her like a second skin and was slit up the right side as far as her thigh. Her hair was up, held in place by titanium chopsticks coated in black lacquer. Stylish and acceptable to security but, with their sharp points, also decent weapons at close quarters. She carried a small clutch purse with a rigid frame made of stainless steel that could double as a small shield.

My worn leather holster hung empty at my right thigh. It was fashionable for men to wear an empty holster or even a short scabbard with formal wear as a symbol of their virility. Most were too small to carry a useful weapon and were embellished with complex inlays of precious metals and jewels. They were fashion statements or displays of the wearer's wealth. Wearing a real, well-used holster made its own sort of statement.

I stepped out of the tube capsule, turned and offered my hand to Cleo. She took it and favored me with one of her dazzling smiles. She'd been against this idea at first, but once we had the invitation and Sam's blessing, she got into the spirit of the affair. She loved dressing up and going out anyway.

We made our way out of the VIP tube stop and a three-wheeled covered car pulled up in front of us.

"Captain Mbele?" The car's AI spoke in a proper Alta Hesperion accent; a man's voice which was a little unusual for AI's. I guess its programmers thought a chauffeur should be male. "I am at your service for the evening. Will you and Ms. Lee be making any stops before our arrival at the Planitia Club?"

"No, we'll go directly to the reception. Do you have a standby and surveillance function?"

"Yes, sir. I can be directed to wait at a specified location, or to respond to a prearranged signal. What do you desire?"

"Wait within line of sight of the club entrance. I'll motion like this"—I held my hand up and moved my arm in a circular motion, the classic infantry recall signal—"when I want you to pick us up. Monitor my link for a voice command."

"Yes, sir. Do you expect to leave the reception precipitously?"

"We'll leave when we decide to leave. Your job is to pick us up." I didn't know how closely these rental transports were monitored by the security services and wasn't about to tell this AI about our business.

"Yes, sir." Its response was carefully neutral, but I got the impression that I'd hurt its feelings. We climbed into the soft contoured seats and the car pulled out into the light traffic and accelerated smoothly.

From somewhere behind us, I thought I heard a faint shout. "*Bai Lianhua!*"

Cleo stiffened and turned to look back at the tube station. I followed her gaze but saw nothing. Her eyes darted back and forth, searching the crowd in front of the station.

"Anyone you know?" I asked.

She shook her head but didn't say anything as she turned back and settled into the seat. She looked composed, but I could feel the tension in her thigh as it pressed against my own.

"*Bai Lianhua*; White Lotus. That name mean anything to you?"

She smiled. "Just someone I knew a long time ago. Not important." She looped her arm through mine and squeezed my elbow. "Let's just enjoy this chance to get out and have fun."

I pressed her arm into my side. "Sure. But stay sharp. We need to find out where these guys have taken Ingrid."

The car joined a line in front of the Planitia Club. Outside the Club, the upper crust of Highpoint swirled and mingled like a flock of brightly jeweled birds. The pecking order shook out into three groups. The merely wealthy strutted and preened on a wide purple carpet fronting the club entrance, seeing and being seen. The powerful clustered to the sides, exchanging polite nods and wary glances, like predators sizing up the competition and choosing their next prey. The real players, dressed in understated shades of black and brown, arrived quietly. They were ushered into the club by anonymous, hard-looking men in dark suits that bulged in places where most people didn't have bulges.

Our car moved forward in the line and stopped in front of the entrance. We stepped out and joined the group of newcomers who now claimed the middle territory of the purple carpet. I offered Cleo my arm, and we moved off to the side where Sam Guthrie waited with the other predators. I felt the eyes of the curious and the hostile follow us as we walked, appraising Cleo and eyeing my empty holster.

Sam lifted a hand and sketched a wave as we approached. Victoria took in my formal wear and the empty holster as well. She looked Cleo up and down and smiled with all the warmth of a Lunar midnight. She took a possessive grip on Sam's arm and leaned close to his shoulder.

"Captain Mbele, Ms. Lee, so good to see you again. I didn't realize you were on the guest list." The warmth in her voice failed to reach her eyes. "Cleo, that dress is absolutely stunning. I just love the old classic look. It never goes out of style."

"Why thank you, Victoria. I'm sure you would know, having experienced so many fashion seasons yourself." Cleo's smile was as dazzling as ever, her teeth sharp and white.

I nodded to Sam, trying to avoid being caught in the crossfire. "Thanks for your help, Sam. We'll make ourselves scarce once we're inside."

Sam shook my hand, ignoring his wife's curious look. "No sweat, Zack. I told you, I'd rather drink with you than waste time with these parasites." He inclined his head toward the colorful crowd milling on the carpet.

"What sort of help did you provide to Captain Mbele, dear?" Victoria slid her arm out of Sam's elbow and edged a pace away from his side. Her voice edged away a lot farther than that.

"Zack and Cleo are here as my guests."

"I see. Whatever you think best." The ice that her husband sold wouldn't melt on her now.

Sam took her by the elbow and pulled her back to his side. She resisted for a second, but gave in. She looked through Cleo and me toward the club entrance where a man in purple livery gently herded the milling crowd toward the door.

"We should go in." Her voice was stainless steel and her eyes blue ice. I figured I wouldn't be on her dance card this evening and felt sorry for Sam. There would be little warmth in his bed tonight.

Sam shrugged slightly at me before tucking her hand under his elbow and starting for the door. Cleo and I followed a few paces behind. Sam wore a full-length scabbard at his side. It was richly tooled leather with brass studs along the seams but was clearly intended to hold a functional blade. Sam was making a statement of his own.

He showed our invitation to the door AI, and we passed through the security scanner. One of the guys in purple livery stepped forward and made a show of searching Cleo's purse but didn't find anything to complain about.

I whispered to Cleo, "Do women always spar like that at these affairs?"

"All the time, darling. All the time. I'm usually not so bitchy, but she rubs me the wrong way. What does Sam see in her?"

I smiled at that. Victoria was beautiful like a hothouse flower, and probably just as expensive to maintain, but she fit right in at affairs like this. And that would have real value to a man like Guthrie whose social skills were on par with Deuce's. She could open doors and smooth over his roughness when clients needed a bit of coddling.

"Love is blind," I said. "I should know."

That earned me a dig in the ribs, but Cleo smiled and gripped my arm in a subtle but affectionate hug.

"Showtime," she said as we stepped through the double doors and entered the club.

The space was not overly large but had been skillfully laid out to give the illusion of roominess despite the presence of sixty or seventy people in it. Soft orchid colored fabric draped the walls and billowed from the ceiling. The bar was dark wood, possibly mahogany, backed by a large mirror. Tables were scattered across a gleaming, blond-colored floor. It looked like wood but, through my boots, it felt like textured plascrete. To the left of the bar stood a compact, raised bandstand, about three meters in diameter on which sat a grand piano. The instrument was finished in a gleaming violet lacquer with gold trim. Across the room from the bandstand, was a raised dais set with a long table. The UB delegation and the local movers and shakers were already seated there, toasting each other with glasses of sparkling wine.

I let Sam move ahead a little. Cleo nudged me and inclined her head toward the bar. Grace was there, in the small space between the piano and the bar, talking to a small man in tailcoat and lace. I started toward her, concerned that the meeting was already taking place, but stopped when the man mounted the bandstand and seated himself behind the piano. He began to play softly. Background music for the arriving guests.

I started walking again. "I think we should get some drinks and let Grace know we're here."

Cleo disengaged her arm. "Just a glass of red wine for me. I'm going to check out the security around the head table and see where the back door is. Just in case."

I nodded and walked casually toward the bar. When I was close enough for Grace to hear, I spoke in a bright casual tone. "Ms. Tyler? I'm Zack Mbele. I heard you perform once on Ceres. I'm looking forward to your set tonight."

She turned to face me with that uncanny ability of hers. "Thank you, that's very kind. I'm glad you could come." She laid a subtle emphasis on the word "glad."

I nodded to the bartender, a real person instead of an AI drink dispenser, and ordered Cleo's wine and neat single malt for myself. I turned to face the room and froze.

Gabriel Zameda stood facing me, about a meter away, a small smile playing across his dark face. He looked elegant in a black tailcoat with brilliant white lace at his throat and cuffs. At his side hung a black leather holster with a single dark blue Tanzanite stone set in the middle. The holster was full-sized and slung low on his thigh, just where his hand could reach it quickly. The Tanzanite winked and sparkled in the light reflecting from the mirror behind the bar. It wasn't the gem that caught my attention, though. The blackened steel hilt of the Steinbauer needler nestled in the holster did that.

"Good evening," he said. He followed my gaze to the Steinbauer, and his smile broadened. "One of the perks of being the head of the security detail tonight."

"Is that official duty? Or are you moonlighting?" I took

a small sip of the Scotch. It was excellent, an eighteen-year-old Laphroaig, dark and smoky. I smiled in return.

"Official duty. The Federal Bureau of Security has been asked to make sure that the Ulan Bator trade minister is well guarded during his stay here."

I saw Cleo approaching from across the room. She stopped when she saw Zameda. Without turning around, he said, "Ask Ms. Lee to join us. I assume the glass of wine is for her."

I wondered for half a second how he knew she was there, and then realized he was facing the mirror behind the bar. I nodded to Cleo, and she walked over to me. She took the wine and sipped it before turning to Zameda.

"Hello, Agent Zameda. And here I thought this was a classy affair."

"Down girl," I said. "Gabriel was just telling me that he's working tonight. Head of security, no less."

Cleo sipped her wine again. "Surely the FBS doesn't expect trouble from this crowd."

Zameda's smile never wavered. "Let's just say that certain parties would be happy to see this negotiation fail."

"No concern of ours," I said. "We're just here to hear Grace sing."

"And where is Mr. Gulbrandsen? I thought he was Ms. Tyler's biggest fan."

I laughed. "Can you imagine Deuce in a room full of people like these? Someone would end up dead."

"Has he killed anyone recently?"

I took another sip of Scotch. Cleo's grip on my arm tightened. "Not to my knowledge."

Zameda leaned closer and lowered his voice. "We found a body on Deck 34, right across from where Mr. Gulbrandsen met with the kidnappers. Shot twice in the gut. Messy business. You wouldn't know anything about the man, would you?"

Somehow, I wasn't surprised that Zameda knew about the meeting, or the body in the vacant storefront. I figured he didn't have any evidence he could use against us, or we wouldn't have walked out of the interrogation rooms.

"Why would I know anything about him?"

"Because he had a black teardrop tattooed at the base of his thumb. I'm told it's the mark of a Martian Black Ops commando. That was your old unit, wasn't it?"

I stiffened in spite of myself. "No. I was Counterinsurgency, Second Special Ops Battalion. Those guys were the First, 'Metternich's Own.' They're supposed to all be dead or locked up with the other war criminals in Antarctica."

Zameda shrugged. "My error. Perhaps he wasn't a real commando; just a *poseur.*"

Cleo gave me a pointed look. I shook my head. I didn't trust Zameda. My nanos and my connection to Metternich had been known to only a few, and most of them were dead.

Zameda watched the exchange with the same knowing smile he always seemed to wear. He reached out and took Cleo's hand, bowing gracefully over it. I'd never been able to pull that off without looking ridiculous. He made the gesture look as natural as walking.

"A pleasure to see you again, Ms. Lee. Enjoy the evening." He nodded to me and walked away toward the dais.

"He knows too much," whispered Cleo. "He's setting us up."

"For what? We haven't done anything yet except crash this reception. If he could prove anything about the guy I shot, I'd already be in a detention cell."

She gulped her wine and set the glass on the bar. "I don't like it. The security detail is full of FBS, paramilitary troops dressed up like private bodyguards. And the back door is covered by two guys in full combat gear. They're expecting some kind of trouble. We should leave."

"We need to see who talks to Grace."

Cleo smiled. "She's tougher than she looks. She can handle the meeting."

"But she can't see who she talks to. We need to ID the contact and get the image to Rabbit. Deuce will be waiting outside to pick the guy up."

Cleo folded her arms and looked stubborn. "It's too neat. Zameda is on to us. He knows who has Ingrid. We should talk to him. Let the Feds handle this."

"We take care of our own." It was my turn to be stubborn. I'd had a gut full of playing the law-abiding businessman. In the five years since I'd owned the *Profit*, I'd built a reputation as a man who was dangerous to cross. I did the job, legally or otherwise, and I got paid. It was easy to be reckless when you had nothing to lose. Being rich and successful had raised the stakes, but what did I have if I let that reputation soften? I'd never be in Guthrie's league, or even Zameda's. All I had of any lasting value was my word and my credibility.

I finished the Scotch and set the glass on the bar. "Come on. I want to talk to Sam before the party gets going."

Cleo stood still for a second, then took my arm with an exasperated sigh and we wound our way across the room to Sam and Victoria. Sam saw us coming and excused himself from a small gathering of Highpoint glitterati and met us halfway.

"What did Special Agent Zameda have to say?" he asked, arching an eyebrow.

"You know Zameda?" I was genuinely surprised.

"His Daddy was my commanding officer during the war. He's one of the richest men in West Africa. The family made a fortune in enriched uranium and rare earth elements back before the war."

Which explains how an FBS agent affords expensive clothes and sidearms, I thought. "That's part of the business you may have to deny knowing about. But why is an FBS agent with family connections in charge of security for this reception? You said yourself it was mostly for show."

Sam nodded. "Yeah, but it's an important show for the Federal Government. The genetics industry around UB wants to build a private LaGrange station for their hot labs. UB used to be the middle of nowhere but, over the last fifty years, has gotten too big to be a comfortable place to play with gene splicing. I just did a deal with the head of Li Gentech to supply ice for the station. That's not public knowledge, by the way, so keep it to yourself."

"Not something I would bring up in casual conversation," I said. "So, who would want to disrupt this cozy deal between the League and UB?"

Sam grew thoughtful. "Any number of Mongolian opposition groups. UB depends on gene splicing; there's not much else there. Moving operations off planet isn't a popular idea around town. But if you're asking who'd be able to make trouble here, I honestly don't know. Maybe the *Si bei Lujing,* the Fourfold Path faction, but I didn't think they had the resources to mount an operation here."

"I thought they were wiped out twenty years ago." The Fourfold Path had been a bunch of natural breeding fanatics who opposed the genetic engineering industry in Mongolia. Twenty-one years ago, they'd assassinated the Prime Minister and tried to take power. The *Federales* put an end to it and locked most of them up in Antarctica long before I joined the military. I didn't know there were any of them left, but then, I'd have said the same thing about the Black Ops commandos.

"So did everybody else, until they blew up a hot lab near Darhan two years ago. They must have had sleepers who avoided being captured. Then some of the leaders either escaped or were released from Antarctica; the stories aren't clear. They've claimed credit for a bunch of low-level assassinations and bombings over the past couple years, but nothing as big as their first job."

"And the FBS thinks they're here?" Cleo scoffed.

Sam looked toward the dais where Zameda was talking with one of his security guys. "Paranoia is a healthy personality trait in some circles."

"And in most circles, it's just insanity." Cleo turned on her heel and stalked back to the bar.

I nodded my thanks to Sam and started after her. Grace stood near the piano up on the bandstand, and the guy at the keyboard had stopped playing. The room lights dimmed, and a spotlight fell on Grace.

"Ladies and Gentlemen," the piano man announced in a deep baritone. "Ms. Grace Tyler!"

Enthusiastic applause filled the room, a minor chord sounded from the piano and Grace lifted her face in the spotlight.

Then all hell broke loose.

Chapter 11

Brilliant light flooded the room followed a fraction of a second later by deep thumping concussions as flash-bang grenades went off near the dais. My nanos opaqued my retinas for the half-second of the flash and then cleared, leaving only a trace of afterburn. Cleo dropped to the floor in front of the stage as the piano man stopped playing and covered his seared eyes with his hands. Grace staggered with the concussion but remained on her feet. She turned this way and that in confusion as automatic weapons fire exploded behind me.

I upended a nearby table and took cover behind it, reaching impotently for my empty holster. There were four men in a line by the door. The security guard who'd checked our invitations lay in a heap behind them. They carried Sikorsky autopneumatics with big sausage-shaped boost cylinders under the barrels and curved, thirty-round magazines in the grips. Two of them started toward the dais, firing in controlled three round bursts. The other two swept the room, not aiming, just forcing everyone to keep their heads down.

One of them saw me peeking around the table and swung his weapon my way. I ducked back and turned toward the bar. The table would stop pneumo rounds but didn't give me much room to move. If I could get behind the bar, I might be able to flank them.

Grace stood by the piano, her shoulders hunched. A spray of slugs thumped into the tabletop behind me. Stray rounds sang past my head and stitched a line up the bar to shatter the mirror behind it.

"Grace, get down," I shouted. Time seemed to slow as my nanos shot into the nerves and muscles of my legs accelerating my reaction time. I dove across the gap between us and knocked her to the floor. She went down hard, twisting her elbow and falling off the low stage to the floor. The purple lacquer finish of the piano splintered as pneumo rounds slammed into it. I rolled to my left and crawled toward the bar, dragging Grace with me.

I tucked Grace behind the relative safety of the heavy bar and started to work my way down its length. Cleo was ahead of me, her clutch purse in one hand like a small shield and one of her hairpins in the other, held low like a dagger.

I snuck another peek over the bar top, my nano-augmented speed too fast for the gunman to see me well. He didn't fire. He was moving slowly toward my end of the bar, still firing short bursts around the room. I caught a glimpse of Zameda kneeling over the body of one of his security guys, firing his needler at the two men who approached the dais. They must have been wearing augment vests or some sort of body armor. Zameda was scoring hits to their bodies, but the needles had no effect.

I hissed at Cleo and she looked my way. I held up one finger and mimed a pistol with the other hand, then pointed to my end of the bar. She nodded. I reached into a bin under the bar top and pulled out a clean beer mug. Not much of a weapon, but I just needed something to throw.

The rate of fire from the two men near the dais slackened. The other two continued to spray long bursts around the room punctuated by brief pauses as they changed magazines.

I took a deep breath and stood up. In an instant, I took in the position of the nearest gunman, the remaining man by the door, and the two by the dais. I yelled and let fly with the beer mug. It struck the man closest to me in the temple, staggering him slightly but not knocking him down. He grinned wickedly and swung the barrel of his pneumatic my way.

I ran to my right as he fired a burst. I was a lot faster than he was, and the pneumo rounds missed, shattering what was left of the mirror and the bottles of fancy liquor lined up in front of it. He corrected, tracking me down the length of the bar. I dove to the floor as slugs sang past my ear and slammed into the bar top.

I turned as Cleo stood and leaped over the bar. I jumped to my feet a couple of meters down from my last position and threw another mug at the gunman, just to keep him focused on me. I almost caught a burst of pneumatic fire in my chest for it, but Cleo reached him just as he pulled the trigger. She chopped downward with her steel clutch bag, breaking his collarbone and throwing his aim off. With her other hand, she drove the lacquered titanium chopstick upward through his back under the twelfth rib. The tip punctured his heart, and he crumpled to the floor; his finger clenched convulsively on the trigger. Pneumatic slugs chewed up the dance floor as he died.

Cleo snatched up the automatic and turned it toward the gunman by the door. The pneumatic booster whined impotently as the empty magazine fed nothing but air into the chamber. She cursed and dropped to her knees next to the dead man, searching his clothes for another magazine. I started toward her as the man by the door took notice and swung his own weapon to cover us. I heard her curse again as she fumbled a fresh magazine out of the man's belt and ejected the spent one from his weapon. She wasn't going to make it.

I dove forward, my nanos pushing my nerves and muscles into overdrive. Cleo lifted the fresh magazine and swung toward the grip of her captured weapon. The gunman raised his automatic. I could see the muzzle coming to bear on Cleo's chest. Then a huge form loomed behind the man. A massive hand grabbed his chin and wrenched his head sideways. The gun fell to the floor at his feet as he was lifted into the air and tossed against the nearest wall like a doll.

The giant Asian stepped into the open room and held out a hand toward Cleo. "*Bai Lianhua,*" he called. Cleo froze, staring at the huge man who had almost crushed my throat down on Deck 34.

"Uncle Po?" Her voice sounded different, more childlike, as she said the name.

She didn't have time to say more. The two remaining gunners, who had finally killed everyone at the head table, turned and noticed the giant and their dead comrade. They opened up on full auto, but the giant was incredibly fast. He tumbled backwards in an improbable reverse shoulder roll and disappeared through the door before the first rounds shredded the orchid wall draperies where he'd been standing.

Cleo spun and fired. Her first burst hit the nearest gunner in the chest. He staggered but didn't go down. He swung his weapon toward her. She dropped him with a carefully aimed headshot. The second one died with one of Zameda's needles in his neck. The dapper Federal agent rose from a crouch behind an upturned table and pointed his needler at the ceiling as he turned toward Cleo.

"Lower your weapon, please, Ms. Lee," he said. "I don't want any misunderstandings here."

Cleo nodded and lowered the automatic. She seemed strangely subdued. She looked past Zameda to the heap of bodies around the dais, then toward the door where the giant had stood. I reached her side and touched her shoulder. She shrugged my hand off and said, "Go check on Grace."

I nodded and stepped back. She continued to stare at the door, her face slack, her hands limp at her sides. I walked slowly toward the bar where Grace now stood, clutching the bar top. This wasn't like Cleo. I'd been in action with her before. She was a cold and efficient fighter. I'd seen her kill a man with a sword and show no more emotion than she did changing her shoes. Come to think of it, I'd seen her get more excited over her shoes.

This passivity was something different. It was like she wasn't there at all. Her body was just holding her place in the here and now, but her eyes were a long way away. Zameda said something to her, but she didn't look at him. He looked at me, but I just shrugged and shook my head.

Grace heard me approach and pulled herself upright to face me. "What's happening?" she asked.

"A bunch of gunmen with automatic weapons and hi-grade body armor shot up the party. It looks like the UB delegation is dead. Are you OK?"

"Scared half out of my wits, shaky, but I'm not hurt. Are you and Cleo all right?"

"Not hurt." I moved around the end of the bar to stand next to her. I touched her arm, and she found my hand. She gripped it tightly for a second. Her skin was cool, and her palm was a little wet, but she seemed composed. I leaned a little closer and asked in a low voice, "Did the kidnappers make contact?"

Her grip tightened convulsively on my hand for a second. "No. In all this chaos, I don't see how anyone could have gotten near me." Her voice broke, just for an instant. "Oh, God. What if the contact was with the UB delegation? What if he's dead? How will we ever find Ingrid?"

I squeezed her hand, not as hard as she had clutched mine, and spoke softly. "Calm down. We have a pretty good idea of where they've taken her. And if their contact was killed, they'll know it soon enough. We weren't responsible for the attack. They'll know that, too, and they won't harm Ingrid. They want us on their side."

"But we don't know where on the Moon they took her. The reservation at the Dai Ichi may not have anything to do with the kidnapping." Grace's voice was edged with panic. She could face gunfire while standing blind and helpless in front of a piano, but the thought of losing her daughter was the only thing that seemed to frighten her. I hadn't shared Cleo's suspicion that Grace was involved in the kidnapping, and this convinced me that she wasn't. She truly feared for Ingrid's safety.

"We'll find her. Their contact may still approach you. Or he may decide it's too risky here and contact you later. Just believe that we will find her."

She didn't say anything, but her breathing slowed, and she nodded once in agreement. I was about to leave her when the piano player stepped close to us.

"You're Mbele, right?"

I nodded. Something about his tone made my nanos tingle. He didn't look like much; a small, neat man with jet-black hair pulled into a tight braid at the nape of his neck. But he spoke with a deep baritone that didn't match his small frame, and his accent was pure Alta Hesperion. He sounded like a newscaster or an emcee for a beauty pageant.

"I was supposed to tell this to Grace, but since it's intended for you..."

He stopped speaking as I grabbed his left wrist and twisted it so I could see the base of his thumb. There was no teardrop tattoo. I spun him around into an arm lock and forced his face into the top of the bar.

"Who are you? Who sent you?" I demanded.

"Wait," he squawked. "I'm just a messenger. They said they'd kill my family. Please, you can't hurt me. They'll kill my kids."

Grace touched my shoulder. "Don't, Zack. Emilio has toured with me for two years. He's not one of them."

I eased the pressure on his arm but didn't let him up. "What's your message?"

He spoke in short grunting sentences, his arm still hurting. "They want to meet with you at the Dai Ichi in Tycho City. Main Lobby, two days from now. 18:00 Lunar Standard."

"Who are 'they'?"

"They didn't say, and I didn't ask. They showed me pictures of my daughters sleeping in their beds. In their own damn beds. They said they could reach out and touch them anytime they wanted."

His voice broke and he stifled a sob. I released his arm and pulled him to his feet. I turned him to face me. "Why should I go to the Dai Ichi? What's in it for me?"

Emilio looked at Grace then at me, a plea in his eyes. I got it. Meet with "them" or never see Ingrid again. Grace got it too. Emilio didn't need to protect her. But maybe he was protecting himself from thinking about what would happen to his daughters if he didn't satisfy "them."

"How are you supposed to contact these people after you deliver the message?"

He shook his head. "I don't know. They said they'd

know if I had done the job, but they didn't say how."

I stood back and looked around the room. They had someone watching us, maybe among the guests, or worse, in the UB delegation. I hoped for Emilio's sake that the watcher was still alive.

Grace reached out and took Emilio's hand as I scanned the room. "It's all right, Emilio. I know you didn't have a choice. I'm sure the girls will be safe."

I nodded in agreement, even though I had my doubts. I waved him away and he scuttled toward the door. I turned to Grace. "Will you be okay here for a few minutes? I need to talk to Cleo and find out if the cops need us to make statements right away."

"I'll be fine. I'm pretty tough for a blind girl."

I grinned. "You are at that. I'll be right back."

Cleo seemed to have come out of her trance by the time I returned to her side. She crouched next to the man she'd killed with her hairpin. She'd opened his collar to reveal the augment vest under his shirt and was turning out his pockets. They were empty. She cleaned the titanium spike on his jacket but didn't put it back into her hair.

"Are you all right?" I asked her. She nodded, but didn't say anything.

I inspected the dead man's face. He was Asian but with broader cheekbones and flatter features than Cleo. He was older than I would have expected. Guys who took missions like this tended to be young. They were full of zeal and ready to die for whatever cause they believed in. Older guys were more invested in living. They wanted an exit strategy.

His equipment was top of the line. The augment vest, an electrostatically charged weave of duraglass nanofibers, was military grade. It would stop a pneumo round or needle and would turn most blades. His autopneumatic was the latest Sikorsky model—built in pneumatic boost, thirty round mag, capable of firing 800 rounds per minute on full auto. When I was in the Special Forces, I'd have killed for gear like this.

"Who the hell are these guys?" I asked, more to myself than to anyone else.

"Maybe you should ask Ms. Lee." I spun around to find Zameda standing over me. I hadn't heard him approach, but Cleo had. She was already on her feet, her hand clenched on the titanium spike.

"What is that supposed to mean?" Cleo's voice was soft, just above a whisper. I recognized the danger in it and stood quickly, placing myself between Cleo and Zameda.

"Easy, Cleo," I said softly in her ear as I gripped her hand and the spike. "Not here, not now. Let's just hear what the man has to say." She tensed against my hand for a brief second but then relaxed. I turned to face Zameda, staying between the two of them in case Cleo lost control again.

"Why would she know anything about these guys?"

Zameda smiled that cold smile of his that never reached his eyes. "If that's how you want to play it, I'll go along. But don't show me a pile of compost and tell me it's diamonds." He nodded toward the body on the floor. "These assassins are Fourfold Path. No one else has the reach or the funding. Look at their features. They're undiluted Mongol, right off the Gobi steppes."

I shrugged. "I wouldn't know. Where I come from, it's what you do that matters, not where you got your genes."

His smile became smug. "Martian Way platitudes? I thought the Revolution was over."

I kept my face impassive but bristled inside at his comment. I had joined the Third Directorate right out of school, a true believer in Metternich's Martian Way philosophy. The Bear had cured me of my religious zeal, but the Way was still embedded deep in my soul.

I no longer believed in the superiority of *Homo astralis*, Metternich's term for the branch of humanity that had adapted to life away from the Mother Planet. But the ethnic purity movements that were sweeping Earth in recent years seemed as bad or worse than anything the Way advocated.

"Why should that concern Cleo?" I asked, controlling an impulse to shove his shiny teeth down his throat.

"I told you not to bullshit me. Mbele." He pointed over my shoulder at Cleo. "Your ex-wife was trained as an assassin by the Fourfold Path. She's been suspected in political assassinations from Tharsis to the Belt. The only reason she's not in a cell in Antarctica is that there's no one left alive to tie her to the killings."

Chapter 12

I opened my mouth to tell Zameda he was the one who was bullshitting, but my augmented hearing picked up a slight sharp intake of breath behind me. I glanced back at Clco. Her face was as impassive as a mask, but her body was rigid, and her heart rate was spiking. *What the hell? I knew she was well trained, but an assassin for the Fourfold Path?*

I turned back to Zameda. I didn't think he noticed Cleo's reaction. He stood still, no longer pointing at her, his head slightly cocked as he watched her for a response.

"You're either drunk or delusional," I said. "Cleo took out two of these guys and probably saved your sorry ass in the bargain. Why would she do that if she was one of them?"

"Come on, Mbele. You should know the answer to that. Wasn't that one of Colonel Metternich's favorite tricks? Shoot one of your own to establish the *bona fides* of your real agent."

I felt a tightening in my forehead and the nanos shot

through my nerves priming my muscles for action. I fought down the urge to grab Zameda by the throat. “Be careful, Agent Zameda. You’re close to a line you don’t want to cross.”

“I know who you people are,” he said quietly, not concerned about the threat in my voice. “I know this isn’t just a social event for you and Ms. Lee. You pressured Guthrie into an invitation so you could make sure no one survived the attack. No loose ends that could be traced back to the people behind this.”

“And why should we care about that? I’d never heard of the Fourfold Path until this evening. I’ve never even been to Earth. So why would I give a shit about a bunch of Mongolian terrorists?”

“Because they kidnapped your friend’s daughter. Ingrid Tyler isn’t on Highpoint anymore, which makes her disappearance a Federal matter.” He held up a hand and ticked points off on his fingers as he spoke. “Lee and Gulbrandsen met with one of the kidnappers in a bar on Deck 34. Twelve hours later, a squatter stumbled onto a body in an empty storefront across from the bar. Forensics puts the time of death at within a few minutes of their meeting in the bar. We haven’t identified the man yet and I can’t place you in that storefront, but the same Asian giant who was here tonight was seen on Deck 34 around the same time as Lee and Gulbrandsen. I don’t believe in coincidences. You’re all involved in this, and Tyler’s little girl is the leverage they used to co-opt you and Gulbrandsen.”

I laughed bitterly at that. “These jokers didn’t take Ingrid. And the people who did are way out of your league. If you think you can tie me to this, go ahead and arrest me. Otherwise, stay out of my way.”

“Don’t push me. I’d love to put you and Cleo Lee in a cell for the rest of the century. But that’d still leave me with a problem." He pointed at the dead man on the floor. "These 'jokers' were sent by someone higher up in the Path. Probably the same someone who took Ingrid Tyler. They've been in contact with you. You're going to follow their directions for getting the girl back, find out who planned this operation, and then you're going tell me who and where they are."

"You really are delusional. If, and I say IF, I find the people who took Ingrid, the last thing I want is you and your storm troopers breathing down my neck. Deuce and I will handle getting her back. You can go pound sand."

Zameda smiled his cold smile again and held out a small, laminated card. "Call me at the com locus on this data card once you've reviewed the situation." He turned and walked away, shouting orders to the surviving security guards.

Cleo grabbed my arm. "Now will you believe me? He knows about us. He knows about the money."

"He seems to know a lot about you, too. How much of what he said is true?"

Her face hardened and her eyes went cold. "Does it matter?"

I thought about that for a second before answering her. "Maybe not. But we need to talk about it if there's anything to it."

She looked away. "Not here. We need to get Grace home. The meeting with the contact is already blown. They may try to get in touch again soon."

"He's already reached out to me. It was Emilio, the piano player." She raised her eyebrow at that. I shrugged. "They threatened his daughters. He's a cutout. He doesn't know anything."

"Then he's as good as dead."

"I hope not. Grace likes him. He delivered his message, so maybe there's no reason to kill him." I knew as I said it that it wasn't likely. Even a cutout might reveal a critical detail to an experienced investigator. Black Ops didn't leave loose ends.

Cleo looked at me like she wanted to say something more, but then just shook her head. "We need to leave before the law shows up. We can't afford to get tied down giving witness statements."

"Right. Get Grace out of here. I need to check on Sam. I'll meet you out front."

She gripped my arm. "Sam can take care of himself. Don't take too long. We've got another two minutes before the first responders show up. Maybe less."

I nodded and she turned toward the bar. I started toward the door, scanning the room for Guthrie. Halfway to the exit, I saw him. He knelt near an upturned table, his arms covered with blood to the elbows, the elegant lace cuffs of his shirt hanging like bunches of red grapes from his wrists. Victoria sat on the floor next to him with her back against the tabletop. Her eyes were wide, staring at the body on the floor near her feet. It was one of the security guards, a guy from the ordinary police detail, not one of Zameda's men.

I hurried across the two or three meters to Guthrie's side and touched him on the shoulder. "Are you hit, Sam?"

He shook his head. "It's not my blood." He held his red-stained hands out toward the body on the floor. "He took a slug for us. He pushed Vickie and me down behind the table and stood over us with his stun baton. Like that was any good against pneumatics." He closed his eyes for a second. When he opened them again, his gaze was cool, the Marine squad leader he had once been replacing the rich businessman he'd become. "Did this have anything to do with your 'deniable' business?"

"No, Sam. I swear. This was as big a surprise to me as anyone. We were here to meet a contact about something else."

"What?"

I glanced toward the door where Cleo stood with Grace. "There's no time right now. Get in touch after the cops debrief you. I'll fill you in."

I started for the door, but he grabbed my arm and stopped me. His voice was calm, like a C.O. issuing orders. "I need you to find the people who did this. I know who you are, who you used to be. Word in the tunnels was that you and your crew were dangerous people to cross. Killers, cold as moon rock. You name your price. I'll write you a blank check. Just make sure someone pays for this man's death."

"Sam, I can't..."

He tightened his grip and cut me off. "Just do it, Zack. I'll bankroll whatever you need."

I pulled away. "Call me when the cops are done with you. No promises."

I caught up with Cleo and Grace at the door. We stepped around a pair of Zameda's security team, dead with neat round holes in their foreheads. They'd been disarmed and forced to kneel in front of the door before they'd been shot.

I tried to picture the scene. The last guests checked and passed through the door, the small knot of curious onlookers starting to disperse, the security detail relaxing a bit, regrouping from gate check to entry surveillance mode. A slight easing of their edge. The four gunmen would have been in a ground car, the windows blacked out, a driver, AI or human, in front. The security guys would have stepped forward, checked the car and maybe moved to open the door. No problem, just a late arrival; until the guns came out. One on one side of the car, a second on the other, getting the drop on them. Quick, efficient and well-rehearsed.

I checked the chronometer in my link. It had been five whole minutes since the shooting started. A terrible response time for a police department as good as Highpoint's. Akira Kensai would never have taken that long. Unless Zameda was slowing things down, giving us time to get clear before the cavalry arrived. That wasn't a thought that gave me much cheer.

I raised my arm and waved my fist in the recall signal. Ten seconds later, our ground car slid up next to the club. Cleo helped Grace into the back and sat next to her. I squeezed into the front. It wasn't designed for passengers but there was room over the maintenance hatch for me to sit, barely. The AI squawked but I told it to shut up and drive toward the south end of the arcology, away from the spaceport.

The Esplanade was a wide boulevard running nearly the length of the arcology. Gleaming towers and glass-fronted shopping malls rose like the shining cliffs of a man-made mountain range to our left. To the right the green swath of the central parklands was an undulating sea of grass and colorful plantings. I kept my head and eyes moving, checking behind and to the sides, automatically falling into surveillance detection mode.

"Turn right up ahead," I told the AI chauffeur. "Cut through the park and find the nearest tube station on the other side."

"Yes, sir. If I may say, sir, your precautions are not necessary. There is no one following this vehicle."

"You have counter surveillance programming?"

"Yes, sir." The tinny voice managed to sound officious. "I am often chartered for diplomatic duties."

"Do you record your counter surveillance sweeps?" I asked.

"Yes, sir. They are on a thirty-minute loop."

I checked the time on my link. It had been only ten

minutes since the shooting started. “Play back the last fifteen minutes of recording, 4 to 1 speed. Send it to my link.” I gave a command to open the link to the AI’s transfer and watched the scene through the contact display in my left eye.

Things went down pretty much as I had surmised. The guards were taken by surprise by the four gunmen, disarmed and shot with professional dispatch. The four readied their weapons and went through the door as a group. I watched for a few seconds more before seeing what I wanted to see. The huge Asian stepped into view about ten seconds after the gunmen entered the club, make it about three quarters of a minute after the takedown of the guards. He bent and checked each man, then grasped them both by their collars and hauled them off the sidewalk and into the alcove of the club. He was out of sight for about another minute, then came tumbling backwards out the door. He looked left, then right and then straight at the camera as if he knew he was being recorded. Then he walked quickly away in the direction of the spaceport.

I activated my link. “Rabbit?”

“Here Zack. Are you okay? It’s all over the nets. There’s been an attack at the Planitia Club. Deuce is gearing up to go out and find Grace. What’s happening? Was it the Revenants?”

“Tell Deuce to stay put. Grace is with us. She’s safe. I need some slicing done. Can you access the AI driving the ground car we’re in?”

“Read me its registration number.”

I checked the display above the windshield and read off a twelve-digit number.

“Got it. What do you want done?”

“Erase the last hour of memory once we leave the vehicle.”

"Sir!" The AI's tone was at once alarmed and indignant. "That is a violation of your rental agreement. I am programmed for absolute discretion. What happens in my passenger compartment stays in my passenger compartment."

I smiled. "I appreciate that. Please let us out at the tube station up ahead. We'll rely on your discretion."

The car swung left out of the park and onto a wide boulevard, a quieter, more residential reflection of the Esplanade. It crossed three lanes of light traffic, mostly personal scooters and ground cars, and slid up to the curb in front of a tube station. I got out and walked around the front of the car to help Grace out of the back. Cleo followed and checked the station entrance before nodding to me and starting down the short ramp to the turnstiles.

I closed the car door and said, "Rabbit, wipe it."

The AI's squawk of protest was cut off as Rabbit dumped its memory. I might have felt badly about lying to the machine if it had been as sophisticated as Sylvia. But even Sylvia was property in the eyes of the law. No AI could refuse an official command to release information, no matter how discreet it promised to be.

Cleo had a capsule waiting by the time Grace and I made it down the ramp to the boarding platform. She keyed in the code for the spaceport and closed the hatch, sending the empty capsule on its way. I helped Grace call another one using her own ID and we climbed in. I set the code for the second stop beyond the spaceport and the capsule slid into the traffic stream and accelerated. I was pretty sure we were all targeted for surveillance but didn't want to make things any easier for Zameda or anyone else.

Two and a half minutes later, we slid to a stop at a crowded shopping area and got out. I spotted the security cameras at either end of the boarding platform and chose a winding path through the crowd that kept them from getting a clear line of sight on any of us. Cleo moved out ahead, keeping up a rapid counter surveillance scan. I had to steer Grace through, although her movements became a lot more fluid as we walked. Again, I was surprised at how well her implants worked, as if she could see, or at least sense, the people around her as she smoothly sidestepped obstacles and waited for rushing shoppers to pass in front of us.

The crowd thinned as we exited the shopping center and headed toward the square fronting the passenger terminals. I began to feel conspicuous in my fancy tails and lace, although no one seemed to be taking notice. Still, a pair of beautiful women in evening dresses was likely to attract some attention. It couldn't be helped, and in truth, I doubted our countermeasures were worth much. Zameda knew where we were docked and so did Ingrid's kidnappers. The mysterious giant might not, but he hadn't seemed to have much trouble finding us after the incident on Deck 34.

Still, it felt good to be back in operational mode. It might not matter here and now, but when we got to the Moon, it would be for real, and security was a matter of constant practice until it became second nature. Playing the respectable charter captain had been stifling me; I hadn't realized how much until the past twenty-four hours. Scanning the crowd in front of the spaceport, following Cleo's lead with my nanos tingling on high alert, I felt more alive than I had in months. I had kicked a jolt habit years before, but sometimes I still missed the initial rush as the drug hit the pleasure centers in my brain. Adrenaline could be a rush, too. I'd been tame for too long.

Chapter 13

"First we find Ingrid, then we kill these bastards." Deuce's voice was a low growl. We were holed up in a cheap hotel a few decks down from the spaceport. It was a place that rented rooms by the hour for 'business' meetings. It had taken all our pooled cash to book three hours, and the human clerk who took our money didn't bat an eye about renting a room to a man in evening clothes with two beautiful women in tow. He'd seen it all. Deuce had come down from the ship, running his own counter surveillance, and now hovered protectively at Grace's side. Rabbit had stayed behind with Sylvia but had sent a portable interface and virtual keyboard along with Deuce.

"Not disagreeing with you, Deuce," I said. "But the guys who shot up the party tonight aren't the people who are holding Ingrid."

"You think I give a shit? Grace coulda been killed."

"I'm with Zack on this one, Deuce." Cleo spoke quietly, but her tone was liquid nitrogen. "I have more reason than you to go after the Fourfold Path, but Ingrid's safety comes first. We can't afford to poke a hornet's nest until she and Grace are out of harm's way." She must have caught a look of surprise from me, because she took a step closer to Grace and said, "I'm sorry I implied you had other motives for being with Deuce. I promise you here and now that I'll do everything I can to get Ingrid home safely."

"I thought you wanted to leave it to the *Federales*," I said.

She glared at me. "So I changed my mind. No one is going to kidnap a little girl and walk away from it. Not if I have anything to say about it."

I held up my hands in surrender. Something had changed her attitude toward Grace and Ingrid. I figured "Uncle Po" had something to do with it, but Cleo didn't seem inclined to explain.

Grace spoke before I could press Cleo for an answer. "Thank you, Cleo. That means a lot to me."

She took Cleo's hand and once again I got the feeling there was some silent understanding being negotiated between the two of them. After a second or two, Cleo nodded and pulled Grace close for a quick embrace, then stepped back and brushed a hand across her eyes.

"So what's our next move, LT?" Deuce asked.

"We have a little over forty hours before we meet with Ingrid's kidnappers at the Dai Ichi Hotel on the Tycho Promenade. I want to get there with enough time for some serious recon and preparation before the meeting goes down."

"Want me to call Mariko and line up some muscle from the Guild Hall?" Mariko was the widow of Deuce's stepbrother, Mike Finney, and unofficial den mother to the Miners Guild in Tycho City. She could call on a dozen tough miners for back up if we needed it.

I shook my head. "No. These guys are ex-commandos. Miners are a tough bunch, but they're no match for a Black Ops squad. Besides, we want to avoid a stand-up fight."

"So what do we do? Walk in and ask 'em 'pretty please' to give Ingrid back? Better a stand-up fight than givin' 'em the advantage. Didn't the Colonel say, 'Hit ' em fast, hit 'em hard, hit 'em often'?"

"That kind of thinking will get Ingrid killed," Cleo said.

Deuce rounded on her. "You got a better idea?"

Grace placed a hand on his shoulder. "Sven, you need to stop and listen. You can't help Ingrid or me if you lose control of yourself."

Deuce clenched his fists until his arms shook but, after a few seconds, the tension in his shoulders eased and he nodded. Cleo didn't speak but looked at me expectantly.

I called the ship over a scrambled frequency through my link. "Sylvia, what's our best time to Tycho?"

She answered immediately. "Twenty hours if we drop below the ecliptic and cut across the shipping lanes. Two hours at ten G acceleration, a mid-course two G bump and then we coast into lunar orbit with a ten G decel at the end."

Commercial shipping tended to stay on the ecliptic and use the free gravity ride of orbital mechanics to maximize drive efficiency. Dropping below the ecliptic mean we could use the *Profit's* drives to bully our way straight across the long curve of the Moon's orbit and get there more quickly. But the cost in wear and tear on the induction coils and reactor would be high. No matter. We'd replace the coils at Port Tycho and pay the fine for a nonstandard flight path.

"Get us a launch clearance as soon as you can."

"Yes, Boss. Should I file a flight plan, or are we running dark?"

Running dark meant turning off our transponder and dropping off the traffic control grid. Dangerous in a shipping lane but safer below the ecliptic. Besides, we'd be in lunar orbit before Highpoint Control could file a complaint. "We'll go dark as soon as we clear the outer beacon."

"Will do."

I keyed Rabbit's link as Sylvia signed off. "Rabbit, I assume you're still tapped into the Tycho security grid. We'll need detailed plans of the Dai Ichi, both the public and the maintenance areas. I want to know every entrance and exit, even the utility shafts."

Before Rabbit could answer, Sylvia interrupted. "Boss? We've got a problem. The Port Authority says our credit draft has been declined. They want cash for the berthing fees before they'll clear us for launch."

I felt a sinking sensation in the pit of my stomach and remembered what Zameda had said when he handed me his data card. "Cleo, check our accounts."

Her face went pale, but she just nodded and activated her link.

"Rabbit," I said. "Can you slice the Port computers and get us a launch clearance?"

"Sure, Zack. It may take a few minutes. But it isn't worth the effort. They'll notice the status change and lock down the bay before we can open the outer doors."

"Damn. Cleo, what about the banks? Can you find out what's going on with our credit?"

"I'm locked out, Zack. The savings, the credit line, the stocks, everything." Her voice was tight with barely controlled anger and a hint of panic. "I told you we were in trouble. Zameda knew too much about us and now he's frozen our assets."

I didn't react to the accusation in her statement. Partly because I knew she was right, and partly because

I was trying to calculate how far we could get without our money. The truth was, not far at all. Without a launch clearance we were bottled up in the cargo bay as tightly as in a plasma bottle. And our cash on hand probably wouldn't cover a good meal, much less the berthing fee for the time we'd dawdled here.

I pulled Zameda's card out of my pocket and activated my link. I read off the comm locus and the link made the connection. He answered immediately.

"Are you ready to talk business now, Mbele?"

I selected the intercom key in my interface so that everyone could hear the conversation. "What do you want, Zameda?"

"No need to be hostile," he said. I held up one finger to silence Cleo when she opened her mouth to respond. Zameda went on, "I told you at the Planitia. I want you to work for the FBS on this Fourfold Path case. I know they were in touch with you before the attack and that they are holding Grace Tyler's daughter to ensure your cooperation."

I could see the anger in Cleo's face replaced by surprise and then a look of colder calculation. Grace looked puzzled but kept silent. Deuce's face was a stone, cold and hard.

"And I told you, I never heard of the Fourfold Path until tonight. Now why have you frozen my accounts?"

"Call it insurance," he said. "Or leverage. Either will work. I told you what I wanted. And I've demonstrated the consequences of refusing."

"How can I do anything when my money is frozen, and my ship is bottled up in the spaceport?" I demanded. "I've got nothing to give you."

"Then we have nothing to talk about," he said.

"Wait!" I shouted before he could break off. "What do you want us to do?"

"I want you to follow orders," he said quietly. "I want

you to follow the kidnappers' instructions but keep me in the loop the entire time. I don't give a fig about the girl as long as I get a lead on the Fourfold Path. Once I have the entire group in custody, I'll release the money."

"What about the port fees and launch clearance?" I asked. "We only have forty hours to get to the Moon and meet these *bautou* at the Dai Ichi."

"Work with me and the port fees will be paid, and the launch clearance issued," said Zameda. "I'll release sufficient operating funds as the case moves forward." He paused. "And when you give me continued updates on the Pathists."

I looked at Cleo who gave a small nod, at Deuce who merely shrugged. Rabbit whispered in my link on the secure comm. "We've got no choice Zack. I can't slice the launch hold without Security knowing about it."

"All right, Zameda," I growled. "We'll play your game."

"Good." There was a pause and a muttered command. "The port fees have been paid. I'll meet you at your ship and we'll release the launch hold."

"What do you mean you'll meet us at the ship?" I asked.

"I'll be going with you," said Zameda. "Wherever you go, I'll be there. I'm not letting the lot of you out of my sight. Not until we take down these animals from the Path."

"That doesn't work, Zameda," I said. "The people who have Ingrid can smell a cop through hull metal. We'll never even get close to them with you tagging along."

"Find a way to make it work, Mbele. I'm sure your pet slicer can keep me in the picture without the bad guys seeing me." He paused for effect. "We don't have time to negotiate here. You're on deadline and I'm out of patience."

I hate being manipulated. Harder cases than Zameda

had tried. They weren't around anymore, and I was. I'd play along because Zameda held all the cards. For now.

"We need thirty minutes," I said. "Don't be late."

"Thirty minutes." Zameda broke the connection.

Cleo started to say something, but I held up a hand. "Give me a minute, Cleo." I spoke Sam Guthrie's number into my link.

He answered right away. "I'm here, Zack."

"Can you talk, Sam?"

"I'm clear. The cops didn't ask many questions and didn't seem to care about my take on the gunmen. They were pro's but older than the usual suicide squad. True believers."

"My impression as well." I was again impressed with Sam's tactical sense. Once a Marine, always a Marine.

"Zack, what the hell's going on here?"

"Quick and dirty, no time for long explanations. Deuce has a daughter, Ingrid. Grace Tyler is her mother. She's six years old and she's been kidnapped. We were at the Planitia to meet a cutout who was relaying the next instruction for getting her back. The attack by the Pathists was a coincidence, not related to the kidnapping. But Agent Zameda knows about Ingrid and thinks we're linked to the Pathists somehow. He's frozen our accounts and locked down the *Profit* to force us to be his informants and help the FBS track down the guys behind the attack on the Planitia Club."

"Who are the guys who took Ingrid? And what do they want with you?" Sam asked. I hesitated and Sam sensed my reluctance. "What, Zack? I just survived a gunfight by hiding behind a table when I should have been fighting back. What's so secret about this bullshit you've landed me in?"

Sam was right to be angry, but this information could get him killed. I sighed. I looked at Deuce and Cleo. He just stared at me, and she gave a slow but clearly reluctant nod.

"What have you heard about Revenants?" I asked.

"Revenants? Metternich zealots roaming the Belt? Boogie men to scare newbies and children."

"They're real, Sam," I said. "Deuce and I have run ops against them twice in the last couple of years."

There was a long silence before Sam said, "*Honto?* If it were anyone but you telling me this, I'd say you were crazy. But why take a six-year-old kid?"

"This is close hold, Sam. If anyone finds out you know this, you and everyone close to you could be at risk. These people won't hesitate to kill anyone they see as a threat."

"I get it, Zack," he answered. "I've made my fortune by knowing how to keep my mouth shut. What do these Revenants want with you and your crew?"

"They're acting on orders from their leader." I paused. *All in or nothing.* "Metternich is still alive, Sam. I've spoken to him myself. He wants me for some special job. I don't know what yet, but he's taken Ingrid to force us to work for him." He gave a harsh laugh. "I'm serious, Sam. I last saw him about a year ago."

"Oh, I believe you, Zack," he said. "It actually explains some of the strange shit that's been going on in the Belt and on Ceres. Odd movements in the markets and deals suddenly gone bad." He sighed. "OK. What do you need from me? I meant what I said about payback for McHenry. That was the security man's name, by the way. Cyrus McHenry."

"I'll make sure the Pathists pay, Sam. But Ingrid comes first," I replied. "Are you still in?"

"I'm in. What do you need?"

"Our money is tied up. I'm sure Zameda plans to dole out just enough for each phase of the operation. That way he controls all of our movements. I need a source of funds he can't touch."

"How much?" Sam's voice was matter-of-fact, as if asking the price of a meal, or a new pair of shoes.

"Fifty thousand yuan for a start," I said.

Sam didn't hesitate. "Done. How do I get the money to you if your accounts are frozen? Do you want cash?"

"No, you'd attract official attention trying to draw that much. Rabbit will get in touch with you with an account number." I knew Rabbit would be monitoring the call. He pinged my link to confirm. "It's an anonymous account at the Hang Sang Bank in Tycho City. We've used it before for business we don't want the tax man to know about."

"Once a smuggler, always a smuggler." Sam laughed. "Rabbit's listening, isn't he? He just pinged me with the account. The money will be waiting by the time you get to Tycho." His voice grew serious. "I want results, Zack."

"Thanks, Sam." He would be patient up to a point. But he didn't get where he was by paying for good wishes. "We won't let you down. I'll update you as I can."

Chapter 14

I had told Zameda we needed 30 minutes. It took us less than ten to go up the two decks to the spaceport and get to our docking bay. Zameda arrived five minutes later along with a couple of gorillas in full battle rattle. He didn't introduce them. He had a travel bag slung over his shoulder.

"I see you arrived early, Mbele," he said. "Shall we go aboard?"

I didn't answer, just eyed the armed operators at his back. They returned my look with cold eyes, neither challenging nor aggressive, just assessing. Something about us must have registered with one of them because he shifted his stance slightly to gain a better firing position and gave me a slight cock of his head, as if to say 'Well?'

I showed him an open palm in what I hoped was a placating gesture. "What's with the escort, Zameda?" I asked.

He smiled. "These are Agents Corwin and Wells." He didn't indicate which was which and that earned a frown from the one who'd squared up on me. "They'll be accompanying us to Tycho City. I'll liaise with the FBS office there for security and these two will return by shuttle to Highpoint."

"Wait a minute, Zameda," I protested. "I didn't agree to you bringing armed agents. I told you, the people we're dealing with will spot you as a Fed in a heartbeat. These guys will stick out like compost on a fancy buffet table."

"Did you really think I'd trust you on your own ship in open space?" The scorn in Zameda's voice made my nanos tingle. I controlled myself. "These two are my insurance that you won't shove me out an airlock and make a run for the Belt as soon as we're outside the Highpoint control zone. Once we get to Tycho and I can set up in the FBS office there, I'll send these agents back here to Highpoint."

Before I could say anything, Cleo surprised me by speaking up. "Berthing will be tight. We only have two charter cabins. The First Class has room for two. The other is smaller but comfortable. And we have Grace to think about. You'll just have to double up."

Zameda smirked. "We'll make do. Now let's get going. You're on a schedule."

I keyed in the code to open the hatch, and we stepped through into the open docking bay. Despite the situation, the sight of the *Profit* made my breath catch for a moment. Sleek and black with gold trim around her cockpit and sally ports, she looked both elegant and deadly. She should. She'd started as a Martian Navy fast interceptor. Now dressed as a high-class charter boat, she exuded understated power and speed. You could dress a predator up, but you couldn't hide her nature. That thought made me glance at Cleo striding confidently beside me.

I hung back so that Zameda was walking ahead of me. One of the armed goons edged up beside me. "I'm Wells," he said softly. "And you're Zachariah Mbele."

"And you're a student of the obvious," I muttered. That earned a chuckle, and I looked sideways at him. He wasn't much to look at with a flat slab of a face, bulbous nose, and deep-set eyes.

"I know about you," he said, his voice just above a whisper. "About your reputation both before and after the war. For what it's worth, I don't like this asshole either, but orders are orders."

"Welcome aboard the *Profit,* Agent Wells," I said. I stood aside and gestured to the sally port. He paused, uncomfortable with me behind him in the narrow hatch. I laughed, point made, and preceded him up the ladder.

We gathered in the cargo bay. Deuce and Grace gravitated to the passageway that led to his quarters. Rabbit looked down from the catwalk but was unusually quiet. He gave me a slight nod to confirm that the money transfer was complete. Cleo moved to the ladder to the second deck, and I joined her there.

The effect was to isolate Zameda and his bodyguards in the center of the bay under clear fields of fire from three directions. Wells came to high alert as did Corwin a half second later. Even Zameda recognized their vulnerability.

I let them twitch for a few seconds. "Welcome aboard the *Profit,* gentlemen."

Cleo climbed the ladder to the second deck and Rabbit rolled away toward the salon. Cleo turned at the top of the ladder and looked down. "If you'll join me up here, we'll work out berthing for the three of you."

"Grace will be stayin' with me," said Deuce. "She won't be needin' a charter cabin." They turned and went aft toward Deuce's workshop.

Zameda and his escort started toward the ladder, but I stepped in their way. "First you stow the hardware." I pointed to the pulse rifles Wells and Corwin carried.

"Forget it, Mbele," said Zameda. "What use is an armed

escort that isn't armed?"

I couldn't see Corwin's reaction, but Wells was suppressing a smile as he unslung his weapon from the chest harness.

"My ship, my rules," I said. "They can keep any blades they have in their kits, but on this ship, all other weapons including needlers and stun batons are stowed in a weapons locker. The crew locker is personally keyed to their DNA. We have a guest locker over there next to the starboard sally port. Stow your gear and set the combination on the lock. Or get off my ship."

Zameda drew his needler and pointed it at me. Corwin raised his pulse rifle, but Wells just shook his head and looked amused.

"Sylvia," I said. "Security lockdown." There were audible clicks as every hatch on the ship was closed and magnetically sealed. The overhead lights went out and were replaced by the dull red glow of the battle lanterns an instant later. Zameda looked about in alarm. Corwin grunted and lowered his rifle. Wells laughed out loud.

"What the hell is this, Mbele?" Zameda demanded.

"Lockdown. This ship is sealed tighter than a plasma bottle. All comms are shut down and jammed. All hatches are magnetically sealed. Until I give the release code, you'll need a laser cutter and about eight hours to get in or out."

Corwin looked around uneasily. Wells laughed again, ejected the powerpack from his pulse rifle and grounded the butt on the deck. Zameda fumed but holstered the needler.

"Stand down," he said to Corwin. He glared at Wells, but the agent just returned his stare. He looked at me. "All right, Mbele. Your ship, your rules."

"Sylvia, release code October 2nd." The lights came back up and the hatches to the cockpit and salon hissed open. I indicated the guest locker with an open palm and watched as they stowed their weapons.

"Thank you," I said in my most polite charter captain voice. "Now if you'll follow me, we'll sort out the berthing situation."

In the end, Zameda took the single cabin and Wells and Corwin doubled up in the larger first-class one. As they passed me in the passageway aft, Wells shot me a crooked grin and a thumbs up behind Zameda's back. I found myself liking the man but didn't forget who he worked for.

I finally joined Cleo in the cabin we shared. She'd changed out of her gown and wore the green jumpsuit she favored when we were underway without a charter. I shrugged out of my tailcoat and tossed it onto a chair.

"What was the lockdown about?" Cleo asked as she picked up my coat and frowned at me. I smiled and took it from her, slinging it onto its hanger and placing it in the armoire.

"Zameda and his boys objected to stowing their weapons in the guest locker." I tugged at my lace collar. "I had to insist."

She came over and helped me undo the collar and cravat. "They're unarmed?"

I placed the lace and the silk cravat back in their box and slid it into a drawer. "I let them keep their blades, but the needlers and pulse rifles are locked up."

"Good." She sat on the bed as I slid out of the dress pants and reached into my locker for my tactical gear, black cargo pants, black shirt and lightweight tactical boots.

"I thought you wanted to avoid pissing Zameda off," I said as I dressed.

"That was before he froze our assets and I still hoped he'd leave us alone." She moved over so I could sit next to her and pull on the boots. "Now, I wouldn't care if he took a long walk out the starboard lock, as long as Rabbit could slice our money free. As it is, we have to play along, but we don't have to make his job easier. And I won't be intimidated on our own ship."

I put my arm around her and drew her close. She leaned into me, and I kissed her forehead. "I'm sorry I didn't listen to you when you tried to warn me about him." She didn't say anything, just leaned her head on my shoulder. I wanted to ask her about her reactions at the Planitia, about the giant she called 'Uncle Po.' Sylvia interrupted before I could say anything.

"The launch hold has been lifted, Boss," she said. "We have clearance to leave. What do you want to do?"

"Get us out of here, Sylvia."

Cleo pulled away and crossed the cabin to one of the chairs facing the holomatrix.

"We'll go dark as soon as we clear the outer beacon."

"You've got it, Boss. Launch in fifteen minutes."

I sat on the bed and cocked an eyebrow at Cleo. "Are we good here?"

She looked away. "We need to talk, but not now. Once we're away from Highpoint and underway, we'll have time."

I nodded. "I'll hold you to that." She turned and glared at me for a second but returned my nod.

I rose and left her in the cabin. Both hatches to the charter cabins were closed, so I made my way forward to the salon. Rabbit was noodling on his virtual keyboard. He looked up and grinned.

"Zameda is going nuts trying to get an outside channel," he said. "I'm blocking his comms."

"Good. Sylvia's taking us out any minute now. Is the money safe?"

Rabbit gave me a pained look. "Of course. The transfer

goes through a series of dummy accounts with individual encryption protocols before it ends up in the real account. It'll be there."

I smiled at him. "Never really doubted you, Rabbit. I'm going forward for the launch. Keep our guests locked down until we're in freefall space."

"You've got it, Zack."

I made my way forward, across the catwalk and swung through the hatch into the cockpit. I settled into the command chair just as the depressurization alerts sounded in the big docking bay. Outgassing started with the usual fading hiss and swirls of condensation as residual vapor hit the cold vacuum of the Outside.

I didn't need to be in the command chair for launch. Sylvia was perfectly capable of taking us out; actually, better at piloting the ship than I was. But I felt better being there and Sylvia knew to wait for me.

"VC 334, *Profit,*" said the tinny voice of the traffic control AI. "Outgassing complete. Standby for outer door retraction."

"Thank you, Highpoint control. VC 334, *Profit* standing by."

The huge outer doors to the docking bay began to slide back into the bulkheads I felt a subtle vibration through the deck, barely perceptible, as the doors locked in the open position.

"VC 334 *Profit,* Highpoint Control. You are clear for launch. Download exit vector to Highpoint beacon on my mark. Mark."

"Highpoint Control, this is VC 334 *Profit;* downloaded and locked. Initiating launch sequence," said Sylvia in her flat official voice. Her tone changed to a warm contralto when she spoke to me. "Ready to go, Boss?"

"Take us out, Sylvia." I settled back into the seat as the bay's big electromagnets shoved the ship out into the

Black. We coasted until the Moss drive initiator flashed green indicating we were outside of the station's artificial gravity field. Sylvia engaged the drive, and we swung smoothly onto the vector that would take us to the outer navigation beacon.

I watched the accelerometer as the Moss drive spun up to 2G's. The ship's inertial dampers easily compensated so there was no sensation of movement. I smiled. Cleo had paid a premium to the Highpoint shipyards for an upgrade to our induction coils and inertial dampers. Couldn't subject the paying customers to any undue G stress, right?

We reached the outer beacon in about ten minutes. Now for the real test of our upgrades. "Once we pass the beacon," I said to Sylvia, "go dark and give me a 10G negative translation. At 10,000 kilometers below the ecliptic, transition to best course for Port Tycho."

"Will do, Zack. How do you want to handle landing clearance? Pop-up or slow transition into the traffic pattern?"

Pop-up would mean activating our transponder with another high-G translation at the end of our run, so we'd suddenly appear on Port Tycho's traffic control system. Technically legal but sure to get us a hard look from Customs. I wasn't worried about that. We weren't smuggling for once and, as long as all weapons were locked down and everyone had proper ID, we'd get a warning and a token fine. Maybe not even that with Zameda on board.

A slow translation meant rising gradually into the normal shipping lanes before entering Port Tycho's zone of control and activating the transponder just before we reached their outer beacon. We'd look just like any other ship in transit to Tycho, but until we activated the transponder, we'd be invisible to other ships. Depending on how thick traffic was, that could be dicey.

"How soon do I have to decide?" I asked.

"No rush. I'll need four hours or so to make the slow translation, so say fifteen hours from now?" Sylvia could have given me a precise answer down to the microsecond, but Rabbit's programming made her almost human in her response.

"Let me take the temperature aft," I said. "I'm inclined toward a pop-up but any time we save in transit could be lost if Customs gives us a hassle. If our esteemed guest has the inclination and the juice to give us cover, that's the way we'll go."

"Ok, Boss. Negative translation in 3,2,1 now." There was a half second of vertigo, like stepping into a drop shaft, before the dampers kicked in with a soft high-pitched whine. The transition to our course for Port Tycho barely registered.

I stayed in the command chair as we settled in for a straight 10G run for the next two hours. Then we'd coast on our built-up velocity until it was time for a course correction. The high acceleration profile let us cut the tangent of the Moon's orbital path, but the decel at the end would put huge stresses on the coils and the *Profit's* hull. The ship could take it, but induction coils were expensive and until Zameda unfroze our accounts or Rabbit could slice into them, we were short of funds. I wasn't going to beg Zameda for money and didn't want to abuse Sam's good will to pay for ship repairs.

I stared into the blackness outside the cockpit canopy. Stars in vacuum are bright but cold, giving no hint of the heat in their hearts. The Black isn't a place of beauty for a tunnel rat like me. It's place of frigid danger, of soul freezing death and vertiginous emptiness. And yet I couldn't tear my eyes away, couldn't avoid staring into the deep.

"You all right, Boss?" Sylvia asked after a long while.

"Fine, Sylvia," I shook my head to clear it. "Just thinking."

"Dangerous habit," she deadpanned, which drew a snort of laughter from me. Her snarky side was too much like Cleo, and I wondered how Rabbit had been able to achieve that bit of programming. Rabbit claimed his open-ended programming actually allowed Sylvia's emotions and personality to evolve independently, but that thought was too disturbing for me to think about.

I stood and turned toward the hatch. "Let me know when we make our course correction. I'll know by then how we'll make our approach."

"Yes, Boss."

Chapter 15

I found Zameda and his boys seated in the salon with Cleo. Rabbit had vacated the compartment, maybe for his own quarters. Zameda came to his feet as soon as I entered.

"What the hell do you mean by blocking my link, Mbele?" he demanded.

"No comms in or out while we're running dark," I said. "I told you, the people we're dealing with will smell a cop from as far away as Tharsis. I don't know how good their signals intelligence is, but I'm not taking any chances with Ingrid's life."

"All well and good until we get to Port Tycho," said Zameda with a condescending smile. "But then, for all your 'running dark' precautions, your transponder signal will tell everyone with access to Traffic Control that you've arrived. What does it matter if these mysterious kidnappers know you're enroute?"

"Rabbit has a bit of slicing magic that will take care of that." I turned to Cleo. "Cleo, would you join me aft? We have some things to discuss."

Her look conveyed both resignation and a hint of apprehension. I thought for a moment she was going to refuse, make some excuse or say she didn't want to leave our 'guests' unsupervised. She just blinked twice and said, "Of course. You gentlemen will please remain in this salon, or in your quarters. The galley isn't open, but the meal dispensers have a fair variety, and we'll only be in transit for a little over eighteen more hours."

She rose and I followed her aft to our cabin. She sat on the bed, and I closed the hatch. She didn't speak, just looked at the deck between her feet. I wanted to demand she tell me what Zameda had meant about her being an assassin, insist she tell me who this giant she called Uncle Po was and why he was following her. I wanted to, but I didn't.

I knew she had a past before we met. I'd decided long ago that it didn't matter. That her infidelities and secret bank accounts didn't matter as long as she stayed with me and didn't betray the ship or the family we'd built around it. Hell, I had my own dark past that I hadn't shared with her. She knew about my time in the Bear, the biotanks and the nanos, but I'd never talked much about what Deuce and I did in the run up to the Revolution. I'd told myself at the time that the things Metternich asked of us had the sanction of a cause, a greater good. I knew in my heart that no cause, no righteous sanction could excuse the betrayals, the lies, the outright killings we'd carried out in service to the Colonel's vision of a free and dominant Mars. So, I stood by the hatch and waited for Cleo to speak first.

After a long minute she looked up at me, defiant. "Aren't you going to say anything?"

"I was waiting for you. Look, Cleo, I'm not going to interrogate you. If there's something Zameda has on you that affects the ship and the rest of us, you need to tell me. Otherwise, I don't care what you may have been before I met you, only what you are now."

Her face softened and she looked down. "It's true what Zameda said about me. It's more complicated than he says, but in the two years before the war I was an operative for the Fourfold Path. I didn't know who I was truly working for until the end, but I carried out ten sanctions in two years, on Earth, Mars, and the Moon. Just before the war, the Feds moved on my handlers and most of the Pathists in Ulan Bator. I was cut loose, free for the first time in my life. I ran. I thought I'd covered my tracks. I thought I'd found a new life. I had a new name, a career, and a reputation when I first met you." She shook her head, still looking at the deck. "I was wrong, and now everything I've done, everything we've built, is at risk."

I crossed to her side and lifted her face to look at me. "It's not the first time we've had everything on the line, Cleo." I cupped her chin when she tried to look away. "Usually it's one of my vacuum-brained schemes that puts the ship at risk. We got accustomed to having money and position. Broke and on the run is when we're at our best." That actually made her laugh.

I sat next to her. "So, you were a wet work agent. That's somehow not all that surprising. But who is this giant you call Uncle Po and what does the Path want with us?"

She pulled back and shifted to face me squarely. "What do you know about me, really?" Her tone was serious, her expression intense.

"I know you're the strongest, smartest woman I've ever known." She made a face, but I pressed on. "You're the best unarmed fighter I've ever seen. Flawless technique and speed that almost matches me when my nanos are active. But I don't know anything about your life before you tried to put a needle into me back on Highpoint a few years ago. And I don't care."

"I'm fast and strong because I was bred to be," she said. "And then trained relentlessly to improve that natural edge." I must have looked puzzled because she sighed and took my hand. "I'm the result of a selective breeding program that's been going on for over a hundred and fifty years. I never knew my parents." She gave a bitter laugh. "For all I know I was decanted from a bottle."

"Then who is Uncle Po?" I asked.

"I'll get to that. I don't remember how many Aunties and Uncles I had growing up. I was moved every few months and a different Auntie would take care of me. Sometimes they taught me—languages or etiquette or how to walk and dress. The Uncles usually taught me fighting techniques or weapons. When I got older, the lessons got harder. Finance and economics, advanced weaponry, basic electronics, and cybernetics. The Aunties got younger, teaching fashion, make-up, dancing, and later sexual techniques and seduction. Uncle Po was the only constant. He'd check on me every week, bring me little presents and sit with me while I recited my lessons. He was the one who moved me from place to place and made sure the new Aunties took care of me." She shook her head and wiped her eyes. "He called me his *Bai Lian Hua*, his White Lotus."

I smiled at that. Calling someone a White Lotus wasn't always the complement it might seem. It meant a woman who appeared pure on the outside but was something else on the inside.

Cleo caught my smile and punched my arm. "Yes, I know what it can mean. And it's true. My looks and the lessons the Auntie's taught me let me mix with the rich and powerful. My first targets were Earth politicians and businesspeople. I didn't question why they needed to die. I didn't even think about that. It was a job. Get in, get out and report to Uncle Po. Those first missions were all choreographed, planned out to the last detail. I followed a script. As I got more experience, they let me plan on my own with their approval. By the time they sent me to the Moon for the first time, I'd just get a target and a time frame. I was on my own as long as the target was eliminated. I think that's when it started."

"What started?" I asked.

"Thoughts, doubts, the feeling that there was more in the Universe than what Uncle Po let me see." She shrugged. "Anyway, I was on Mars, in Tharsis, just before the war when the *Federales* rolled up most of the Fourfold Path including Uncle Po. I finished my job and found myself stranded. No contacts, no money, no new orders. That's when it hit me. I was free."

"You changed your name and went freelance," I said. "How'd you get off Mars? We had immigration locked down by then."

"My target was in the Third Directorate. Part of the package was to recover IDs and DNA prints that the Path had created for operations in the Belt. The courier was picked up in Planitia during a raid on a pod flop where he was staying. Wrong place, wrong time. But the officer in charge recognized what the courier had. The courier disappeared and the IDs went up for sale to the highest bidder." She smiled and touched my cheek. "I shot him in the head, helped myself to one of the IDs, and became Cleopatra Lee."

"You took out Morenci?" I laughed. "You did me and Deuce a favor. He was at the top of our hit list after Metternich's coup deposed the Governor." I grew serious again. "So how did the Path find you again?"

"I don't think they have," she said with a shake of her head. "If they had, those *bao e ren* at the Planitia would have targeted me, too. Uncle Po took out the two at the door, so he wasn't part of the attack."

"He's working on his own? How did Uncle Po find you? And why is he looking for you?"

Cleo shrugged. "I don't know. I guess I haven't covered my tracks as well as I thought."

"Since you joined me, we haven't been invisible. Just the opposite. We made a reputation as serious operators, 'stone cold killers' as Sam said. We leveraged that reputation to build up this business. If someone wanted to find you, they probably could." I pulled her to her feet. "Unless Uncle Po has access to some serious intel capability, he'll have a hard time following us to Tycho, especially with Rabbit on board. Once we get Ingrid back, we'll figure out what to do about the Path."

"Rabbit has some slicing magic, I assume?" I nodded and she took my arm. "We need to get back to our 'guests' before they get up to some mischief."

Chapter 16

Zameda and the boys sat around the dining table in the salon looking annoyed. Actually, Zameda looked annoyed. Corwin looked bored and Wells smiled faintly as he watched his boss fume.

He's not happy with whatever game Zameda is running, I thought, watching Wells. *Have to remember that. It could be useful.*

Zameda swept to his feet as Cleo and I entered. "We need to have a conversation, Mbele. You forget who controls your money, and your precious ship. What are you up to?"

"You may control our money, Zameda, but I'm still captain of this ship." My tone of voice made Wells sit up and frown. Corwin reached to his right hip where I assumed he concealed a blade. I half turned to face them. "Stand down, boys. Just making sure your boss understands the current situation."

"And what do you think that is?" Zameda sneered. "I know you won't toss me out an airlock. The FBS knows I left Highpoint on your ship. Once we reach Tycho, I'll hold all the cards. So go ahead, enjoy yourself, 'Captain.'"

I held his eyes until he broke and looked away. "I'm captain of this ship, and as long as you're in her, you'll do what I say. You can leave any time, now or when we get to Tycho. Don't make the mistake of thinking you control me. You control my money and the minute I decide I don't give a damn about that you can eat shit and die." I smiled so he would know I meant it. We continued to glare at each other until Cleo stepped between us.

"Gentlemen," Cleo spoke into the awkward silence. "We need to consider what we'll do once we reach Tycho City. We have different priorities, but we need to work together if we're going to get Ingrid back and shut down the Path. So how can we help each other?"

Both Wells and Corwin relaxed, or at least came down off high alert. Zameda looked from Cleo to me before giving a terse nod. Cleo gestured toward the lounge area, and we found seats, Zameda in one of the active contour chairs and Cleo and I on the sofa facing him.

"I want eyes and ears on your meeting with the Path," said Zameda. "Conejo can make that happen. I know how good he is."

"Rabbit's good, but not omnipotent," I said. "Any surveillance can be blocked, or at least detected. And if these people detect any kind of surveillance, they'll bolt and kill Ingrid."

"How do you know so much about these Pathists?" Zameda pointed at Cleo. "Have they contacted you? Are you working for them again?"

Cleo's face reddened, but she spoke calmly. "The people who have Ingrid aren't the Fourfold Path. They're something much worse."

"Who are these mysterious kidnappers, then?" he scoffed. "You keep talking about these formidable operators but don't offer any solid information."

Cleo shook her head. "You won't believe us if we tell you. Just know that we've operated against them at least twice in the last couple of years. They're real and they make you and your FBS reaction force look like amateurs."

Zameda laughed. "Next, you'll be telling me they're Martian Spec Ops Revenants working for a resurrected Colonel Metternich. Save it. I don't believe in fairy tales."

He stopped as he saw the look on Cleo's face. She held his eye and raised an eyebrow. He looked at me. I shrugged.

"You people are serious. You're delusional. What makes you think these are Revenants?"

"You're a hot shot Fed," I said quietly. "Don't tell me you haven't gotten reports pointing to a group of ex-Spec Ops soldiers operating in the Belt."

"Sure, there's intel but it's mostly rumor and secondary source stuff," Zameda's tone was now serious. "Nothing actionable."

"Think back. A little over three years. You were on Highpoint by then, right?"

Zameda nodded.

"Remember a report of a running gun battle on deck 20? Service deck under the spaceport. Half a dozen heavily armed men."

"But no bodies were ever found. So what?" He folded his arms, but his eyes didn't match his confident tone.

"Akira Kensai knew who they were. Some of them killed a customs team and were trying to cut their way into this ship when Deuce and I took them out. Akira saw the black teardrops on their wrists, right under their right thumbs."

Zameda frowned and his eyes narrowed. "How do you know what Kensai put in his report? That incident is under FBS seal."

"I was there, remember? The Black Ops team was there to take out me and my people because of what we knew about Fingol Malloy." I paused as he thought about that. "A few days later there was another incident, this time on Mars, at Tharsis Docks. Another heavily armed team attacked a ship but were beaten back. The team and all their dead and wounded vanished like ice in a Martian spring."

"And you're telling me these were Martian Spec Ops Revenants," said Zameda. "How can you be so sure?"

"I used to work for Metternich. I recognized some of them. I saw the tattoos. There's no doubt who they were."

Zameda looked from me to Cleo. "Let's say I buy all this, about the Revenants," he said quietly. "Why would they take Gulbrandsen's daughter?"

"They're after me," I said. "They know I'll do whatever they ask as long as they have Ingrid."

"And why you?" Zameda asked.

I considered how much to tell Zameda about my nanos, the Colonel, and the complicated dance of my life since the Revolution. I decided he didn't need a long story, just a believable one. "Deuce and I were part of a Special Forces unit that reported directly to Colonel Metternich. But we fell from grace, and I ended up in Brunault prison for the duration. Deuce got clear and hid out in the Belt. We were both cleared by the Reconciliation Court after the war. Most of the Revenants are still wanted for war crimes. They probably need us for a job they can't do without risking being recognized."

"Job." Zameda's tone dripped sarcasm. "Crime you mean."

"Maybe. Probably." I shrugged at his continued skepticism. "I don't know what they want, but they specifically mentioned Deuce and knew his rank in the Third Directorate. There are only a few people who would know that and most of them are aboard this ship."

"Meaning?"

"Meaning these people, whoever they are, have access to secret Third Directorate records from before the war. Think, Gabriel." He bristled at my use of his given name, but it had the effect I was looking for. "Who would have access like that? Who would know Deuce's rank and real name, much less that he had a daughter. Hell, I didn't know that until a day ago."

I didn't mention Grace's connection to Metternich and the Third Directorate. No need to arouse his suspicions there. I could see him thinking this over.

"What has this got to do with the Fourfold Path?" he asked.

"I don't know," I said honestly. "Other than Cleo's past history with them, I don't see how they fit into the kidnapping. We didn't know about the reception until after Ingrid was taken and, even then, wouldn't have been there if I hadn't called in a favor from Sam Guthrie."

"I almost believe you," said Zameda. "But that doesn't change my position. Cleopatra Lee is my best lead to finding the Pathists who assassinated the UB delegation. If they're not linked to your mysterious Revenants, then this trip to Tycho is a waste of time."

A thought occurred to me, a piece of this crazy puzzle I'd missed before. "Why was Deuce part of an FBS investigation?"

"I can't discuss that," said Zameda, not meeting my eye.

"You weren't watching Deuce, you were watching Grace." Zameda's face told me I was right. "You knew she worked for the Third Directorate. If you don't believe us about the Revenants, why were you watching her?"

Zameda sighed. "We knew former elements of the Directorate were operating criminal enterprises all through the system, but we had no evidence they were coordinating with each other. Then Ms. Tyler was seen in the company of Damien Holtz, a former Major in Martian Intelligence before the war. Since Reunification he's been a facilitator of sorts, acting as a go-between for the Red Dragons, the Kwai Consortium, and various dissident groups on Earth, including the Fourfold Path."

"Holtz?" I laughed bitterly. "He wasn't just a 'Major.' He commanded the death squads. He's a true believer, cold as moon rock and totally committed to the Martian Way." Another piece fell into place. If Holtz was running Grace as an asset, Metternich himself was involved. I had no doubt that he'd be waiting for us when we got to Tycho.

"Whatever he was in the past, it's his connection to the Path that matters to me," said Zameda.

"Holtz is a professional, whatever his business. You won't connect him with the Path, or any of his so-called clients." I shook my head. *How could a senior operative be so obtuse?* "Once we meet with Ingrid's kidnappers on the Promenade and figure out what they want, we'll look for a connection to the Path."

"And I still want a presence at that meeting," insisted Zameda.

I clenched my jaw, activating my link. "Are you getting this, Rabbit?" I asked subvocally.

"You bet, Zack. And yes, I can get him in. Audio at least, vid maybe depending on the quality of their jamming."

I watched Zameda's face. If he suspected that Rabbit was listening in, he concealed it well. "I'll check with Rabbit; see what he can do," I said. "No promises."

"Just make it happen," said Zameda.

"What about cash?" Cleo asked. "We can't simply stroll onto the Promenade in our working clothes. We'll need to look the part, like we belong, or security will chuck us out faster than yesterday's garbage."

"Never fear." Zameda's tone shifted to condescension. "As soon as I contact the FBS office in Tycho, I'll release sufficient funds for you to get a new outfit."

Zameda may have been oblivious to the look of cold hatred in Cleo's eyes, but Wells didn't miss it. He started out of his chair but settled back when I gave him a palms down sign. "It'll take more than just looking the part, Gabriel." I laid a hand on Cleo's thigh and could feel the tension in it. "We need flash money; we may need to spread some cash just to get into the hotel. This is our turf. We'll have an image here that people will expect to see."

Zameda waved a hand dismissively. "How much?"

"Five thousand to start, then we'll see what these *bao tu* want." I rose and offered Cleo my hand.

She took it and stood, murmuring in my ear, "He's a dead man. As soon as this is over."

We left Zameda and the boys looking over the selections from the meal dispenser.

Chapter 17

I dropped Cleo off in our cabin to contemplate creative murder strategies and made my way forward to the cockpit. “Time to course change, Sylvia?”

“Ten hours, twenty-two minutes for slow translation with a five G deceleration profile; twelve hours and forty-five minutes for pop-up with a twelve-point-five G profile.” She lowered her voice, even though I was the only one in the cockpit. “Are you going to space that FBS asshole?”

“What? No! What gave you that idea?”

“Well, after the way he insulted Cleo and the freeze he placed on our money, he deserves it.” Her voice switched to the officious tone she used when relaying information. “I did some checking in the Federation legal code. Zameda has no authority to freeze our assets, and we can report him to their Professional Standards Office for abuse of his authority.” She paused. “Or we can just space him.”

I laughed. “No, we can’t just chuck him out an airlock. We may need him. Still, I don’t trust him and don’t want to ask any favors. I think he’s willing to believe in a bunch of rogue Black Ops commandos operating out of the Belt, but Metternich is an orbit too far for him."

"So, what's our approach plan, Boss?"

I slid into the command chair and punched up the two deceleration profiles. I ran some quick diagnostics on the induction coils and figured they could take the strain of a high G transition. But there was still the possibility of a Customs beef.

"Slow transition, Sylvia. Get with Rabbit and have him slice the transponder. I think we'll use the *Kokopelli* identity this time. We haven't played that one in a couple of years."

"Will do, Zack. Transition in ten hours, nineteen minutes."

"Get Deuce on the com for me, please." He and Grace hadn't stirred from his quarters since we came aboard. I was happy for them but wanted to update Deuce on our approach and let him know that Zameda knew about Grace and Holtz.

Deuce answered on the third chime. "What's up, LT?"

"Just a heads up," I kept my tone light. "Transition to Tycho insertion in a little over ten hours, so you've time to eat and get some sleep. I'd avoid the salon for a while, though. Zameda and his boys are in there and they're not too happy with us right now."

Deuce chuckled. "Want I should go up and sweet talk them a bit?"

"That's exactly what I don't want you to do." I filled him in on our talk and the fact that Zameda knew about Grace's connection to Holtz.

"Understood, LT. But I don't see why we don't just toss that asshole out the starboard lock and be done with him."

I sighed. "Sylvia says the same thing." She emitted a wet sounding raspberry from the cockpit speakers.

"I heard that," said Deuce. "Maybe you ought'a listen to your crew, Cap'n."

"Maybe, but those agents with him probably wouldn't go along, and they're just soldiers doing a job. I don't want to have to kill them, too."

"That guy Wells is sharp." Deuce said. "And he's not happy with his boss. We might could use that."

Deuce might speak like a Utopia Planitia backcountry rube, but he was one of the sharpest operators I'd ever known. "My thoughts too. Stay sharp."

"Always, LT."

I sat in the cockpit for a while, watching the stars. Sylvia picked up on my mood and didn't try to talk to me. After an hour or so my eyelids drooped, and I decided to go back to the cabin. The lights were turned down and Cleo was already in bed reading on her link. I undressed and joined her. By mutual consent, we turned out the bedside light and went to sleep.

I managed six hours before my eyes snapped open, and I came wide awake. Cleo's soft even breathing told me she was still asleep. I couldn't say what had jolted me awake. A sound? I listened carefully but heard only the hiss of the air handlers and CO2 scrubbers and the low hum of the reactor. The Moss drive was shut down as we coasted toward our transition point. I eased out of bed and slipped into a pair of exercise shorts. I picked up my needler from the bedside table and approached the closed hatch.

I listened again with my ear next to the hatch coaming. Nothing. I opened my link to the cockpit. "Sylvia," I said subvocally. "Status report."

"On course and on time, Zack. Two hours and seventeen minutes to transition. All systems checking in as nominal."

"I thought I heard something outside our cabin. Where

are our guests?"

There was a brief pause before Sylvia responded. "Zameda is in the second-class cabin, asleep by his pulse and respiratory rate. Wells is also asleep in the large cabin. Corwin's bunk appears occupied on visual but thermal and audio indicate it's just bundled bedding."

"Shit." I palmed the hatch, and it slid open. "Is there any other movement aboard?"

"Checking. Yes, there's someone down on the main deck. They're under the catwalk, so I don't have a direct visual. They're over by the weapons lockers. Based on audio analysis of breath sounds and weight on the deck plates, it's Corwin."

"Override the combination on the guest locker," I ordered. "I don't want him getting a weapon."

"Done."

I made my way down the passageway, past the guest cabins and the open double-wide salon hatch. The gallery above the cargo bay and the catwalk to the cockpit were in deep shadow. A night light illuminated the ladder and the more passenger friendly ramps that led down to the main deck, but the rest of the bay, including the lockers, remained dark.

I heard him down there, pressing the combination into the keypad, doing it again and yet again. I let him get good and frustrated before saying, "Lights Sylvia."

She flashed the cargo bay lights on at full intensity. They were set at the base of the catwalk, so I wasn't quite blinded, but I did squint. Corwin threw up his arm to cover his eyes and dropped into a crouch. He at least remembered that much of his training. He groped at his hip where his sidearm would normally ride but came up empty. He reached for his boot where he kept a blade. My vision cleared, and I double tapped him in the neck with a pair of sleeper needles.

"Sylvia! Roust Zameda out of bed. Tell him I want him down on the main deck or I'll toss his man out the starboard lock." I made my way to the ladder, hooked my heels on the handrails and slid down to the main deck landing lightly on my toes. Despite my threat to space Corwin, I felt good, almost happy. I thumbed the lock on the crew locker and drew out a pair of flex cuffs. I looped them around Corwin's wrists and cinched them up.

Deuce stepped into the light from the aft passageway. "Trouble, LT?"

"Not anymore, Deuce." I looked down at Corwin and a thought occurred to me. "Do you have one of those UV light sticks back in the workshop?" I knew he used UV light to track drive coolant leaks. Coolant was colorless but fluoresced under UV.

"Sure, LT," he said, puzzled at first but then he looked at Corwin's flexcuffed wrists. "You think?"

I shrugged. "Don't know but suspect it."

Deuce nodded and ducked back into the passageway just as Zameda appeared on the gallery above. He took in Corwin on the deck, cuffed, me standing over him and the needler in my right hand. He rushed to the ladder and did a credible job sliding down.

"What the hell, Mbele," he sputtered. "What did you do to that man? And why is he cuffed?"

"He disobeyed my orders about weapons aboard this ship." I kept my tone matter of fact, reasonable. "He's fine; a couple of sleeper needles in him. He's cuffed for my protection, and maybe yours."

"Are you serious?" Zameda pointed down at Corwin. "Agent Corwin is a decorated veteran. He's been on this detail since the beginning."

Deuce returned at that moment. He said nothing, just handed me a small light stick and withdrew. I faced Zameda.

"Your decorated veteran was trying to open the guest locker, going for a weapon, despite my orders to the contrary. I could space him right now. In fact, if what I suspect is true, I should." I pointed to his wrist. "Corwin likely isn't his name. He's a Black Ops commando, one of Metternich's Own."

Zameda took a step back, head cocked. "You're obsessed with this fairy tale, Mbele. What evidence do you have?"

I clicked on the light stick and rolled Corwin's hand so the UV light shone on his wrist at the base of his right thumb. The teardrop that I had anticipated finding there glowed with soft green phosphorescence.

"What the hell?" Zameda repeated more softly.

"The ink used for the Black Ops tattoo has a phosphorescent component. Security measure." I reached down and turned Corwin's wrist, so the glowing mark stood out. "You can laser off the black, but the phosphor is a vital dye. It stays in the basal skin cells forever."

Zameda stared at the teardrop for a long moment. "I've known this man for two years. Had him on half a dozen operations. There's nothing in his file about a Third Directorate background."

"He's a sleeper, probably placed before the War. You wouldn't know it until he was activated."

"Shit," Zameda swore softly. "He wasn't the first assignment for this detail. The original agent was reassigned at the last minute."

"Watch your back around the person who made that reassignment," I said. "At best, they're compromised somehow. At worst they're part of the group." I didn't mention Metternich. Zameda was coming around, but if I told him the Colonel was still alive, still in control, he'd balk.

"You were right, Mbele." Zameda straightened and

squared his shoulders. “These Revenants are real. I’ll even concede that they’re the ones who took Gulbrandsen’s daughter. But what do they have to do with the Path?”

“Why do you think the two are related?”

Zameda pointed to Corwin. “He’s one of them. Someone manipulated my system to get him assigned to this detail. Why would they do that?”

I started to dismiss the question but stopped. He had a point. “They wanted to keep an eye on you, on the progress of your investigation.”

“But why?” Zameda looked genuinely puzzled. “I’m looking for Pathist terrorists. I didn’t even believe in an organized Black Ops group. Why monitor this operation?”

It occurred to me that there might be convergence in the goals of the Fourfold Path and Colonel Metternich. A marriage of convenience, perhaps. But I still didn’t trust Zameda enough to share that with him.

“Likely some business between the two groups. There’s little honor among thieves. They’d want to know if you were close enough to blow the deal.”

Zameda cocked his head doubtfully. “Maybe. Makes as much sense as anything.”

I pointed to Corwin. “What should I do with him? Personally, I’d have no problem pushing him out an airlock, but he might have some use to you.”

“Keep him restrained until we reach Tycho. I’ll turn him over to the FBS there for questioning.” Zameda turned and made his way to the ladder. “I’ll wait until we’re in the spaceport before contacting them. I think your stealth precautions may be a good idea, after all.”

Chapter 18

Two hours later we transitioned up into the normal shipping lanes. For once we got lucky. Traffic was heavy enough that we could blend in but not so thick that we had to dodge and weave to avoid a collision. Sylvia slid us in behind a big composite freighter and switched on our transponder just inside the limit of Tycho traffic control. To them it looked as if we'd been shadowed by the bigger ship until we were inside the zone of control.

"VC 586 *Kokopelli*, this is Tycho Control. Maintain your current course and hold at the inner marker."

"Tycho Control, VC 586 *Kokopelli,* maintain course and hold at the inner marker, aye," Sylvia replied.

Rabbit had sliced our transponder. As far as Tycho or anyone else was concerned we were now a small corporate liner for Navajo Freight Lines transporting executives and high value goods between Highpoint and the Moon. We'd built the identity during our smuggling days and hadn't used it in a while, but it seemed to be holding.

Forty-five minutes later, we touched down on a

visitor's pad outside the main dome. We paid the standard docking and shore power fees but declined hook-up to TychoNet, the local link service. We'd use our own secure coms piggybacked onto our resident account. We had a permanent berth inside the dome under our own ID, but if anyone actually looked us up, the *Kokopelli* legend would be blown.

One of the improvements Cleo had made with the upgrade to the charter boat was a pressurized ground transport. Our old three wheeled hauler was open; fine inside Tycho but required pressure suits for Outside. The new ground car could seat four in air-conditioned, pressurized comfort.

It took two trips to get everyone through the commercial lock. I left Deuce and Rabbit to watch Corwin while Cleo and I drove Grace, Zameda, and Wells to the spaceport. Five was a squeeze, so Grace and Cleo had to double up in the front passenger seat, but it was only a ten-minute ride. I sent Cleo back to fetch the others.

"Make sure he transfers the money," Cleo said as she slid over to the driver's seat and jerked a thumb at Zameda. She sealed the door and drove off before he could respond.

By the time Cleo returned twenty-five minutes later, Zameda had contacted the local FBS office, transferred five thousand *yuan* to a pay as you go account, and sent Wells to round up a security detail to take Corwin into custody.

Cleo rolled up with Rabbit's power chair strapped to the luggage rack on the rear of the car and Rabbit in the front seat. Deuce sat in the back with a big hand gripping Corwin's shoulder. Corwin was awake but pale and glassy eyed with the aftereffects of Zoldipine. Deuce climbed out and dragged Corwin after him, leaving him to slump to the ground against the rear wheel of the ground car.

Deuce embraced Grace in a gentle hug before lifting Rabbit's chair down and powering it up. Rabbit swung himself smoothly out of the car and into the chair. He rolled over to me, waiting until Zameda moved away to check on Corwin. He reached up and handed me a data stick.

"Guthrie's money is at the Hang Sang, account number is Cleo's birthday, password is Planitia. That's the account key."

"Thanks, Rabbit. We'll head out as soon as Zameda gets his shit together."

We drew together in a small knot around Rabbit's chair while Zameda stood over Corwin. To Zameda's credit, he didn't try to interrogate Corwin right there. Only stood looking down at him with his hand on his needler. Corwin was still glassy-eyed but obviously in control of himself again. He sat still, staring straight ahead.

A minute later, Wells pulled up in a security van with a couple of armed FBS agents in tow. They quickly bundled Corwin into the back. Wells made to get in, but Zameda stopped him with a hand on his arm.

"Wait," said Zameda. "I want you to escort our friends here to wherever they intend to stay until it's time for the meeting. I need to interrogate Corwin. Stay in touch over the link." He turned to me. "Have Conejo link me into your net as soon as you get settled. I want eyes and ears on this meeting."

"That may not be possible," I answered. "Rabbit's good, but any signal can be blocked with sophisticated enough jammers. We can't guarantee we'll stay in touch."

"That's why you're taking Wells along." He raised a hand when I started to protest. "I heard what you said before, and I don't care. Figure out a way to make it work." He turned and climbed into the van. He pointed and the driver spun the steering yoke and turned the vehicle in a tight arc around us.

Wells watched them go, then muttered, "Asshole." I cocked my head at him, and he shrugged. "You heard the man. I guess you're stuck with me."

"Not fond of your boss?"

"No, but I do have my orders," he said. "I don't have to like the man."

"Understood," I said. "Just hoping you can use a little discretion in how you carry them out."

Rabbit ordered up a ground car that would accommodate all of us and looked at me with his eyebrows raised.

"The Blue Booby," I said, and he grinned.

The Booby was a bar on the edge of the commercial port. We had a history there, Deuce and Rabbit and I. True, Deuce had killed Vassa, the previous owner, with a crossbow the last time we'd been there, but the new owner didn't know about that. The bar was close to one of the secure lifts to the Promenade, not one near the Dai Ichi, which was just as well. It also made a good place to gather and plan our approach to the kidnappers. The clientele weren't the curious types, so we'd be reasonably secure.

We rolled down Armstrong Boulevard past the shops and clubs that catered to those with enough money to buy a good time but not enough to pass muster up on the Promenade. Near the entrance to the commercial spaceport, we turned down a narrow alley that ended in an open area about twenty meters across. Nestled between the rocky wall of Tycho crater and the fence to the commercial port stood a low building patched together from old cargo containers and duroplast panels. Centered over the roofline, a cartoon bird with blue feet and a leering grin on its blue beak cupped two buxom waitresses with its broad wings. This was the Blue Booby.

I pushed open the aluminum saloon-style swinging doors and we entered as a group. Durkin looked up from his place behind the bar, saw us, and took a step backward, his face pale. Deuce and I had met him once just after the refit on the *Profit*. We'd come in to pay off a few debts to some less than savory characters. Said characters had treated us with due deference and respect, which Durkin took to mean we were bigger bad asses than they were. I smiled and gave him a two-finger salute.

"Just here to have a drink, Durkin, no fear." He glanced to his left where Vassa had kept a short barrel pulse rifle. Apparently, Durkin had followed his lead. I shook a finger at him, and he held his hand up waist high, palm out.

We found a table near the door to the back room, where private meetings could be arranged. Durkin had renovated, replacing the worn red door with a faux wooden one, and offsetting the dance stage to the left so there were more seats for patrons who wanted to watch the dancers. No one was on stage as we sat down, and the lights were dim. Too early I supposed.

"Everyone listen closely," I said. "We're almost eight hours early for the meeting with Ingrid's kidnappers. I don't doubt that we're dealing with the same Black Ops shitheads we fought before and it's certain the Colonel is behind this. Whether he's here, or just sent his lackeys, remains to be seen. I'm also reasonably certain we're still operationally secure. We'd have picked up a tail at the spaceport if the *Kokopelli* identity was blown. That gives us an edge." I turned to Wells. "I need to know where you stand, Wells. From here on out we're going dark. We have resources your boss can't know about, at least not until this is over. Can you keep that to yourself, or do you walk away right now, no harm, no foul."

"Never liked the way Zameda pressured you into this," said Wells. "Whatever you've got here is none of my business."

I nodded and turned to Cleo, handing her the Hang Sang key. "We need a base other than this bar. Swing by the bank and draw twenty thousand from the money Sam put up. Use it to get us a suite at the Apollo on south Chandra Street and use the card Zameda gave us to buy some clothes that'll pass fashion scrutiny up on the promenade. Take Grace and Rabbit with you. Deuce, Wells, and I will recon the Dai Ichi."

She cocked her head. "Dressed like that? You won't get past the dropshafts."

"Deuce, can Mariko get us some sort of coveralls from her miner pals? Something that'll pass us as maintenance staff?" I asked.

Deuce grinned. "I can do better than that, LT. I've still got those Global Utilities coveralls we used for the Jones operation we ran two years ago. Got badges and everything. Conejo may need to update the cert's on 'em but they should get us into the freight and maintenance spaces."

"Back at the ship?"

"Nah," Deuce shook his head. "Got 'em in a private locker at the commercial port along with my old Nakagima pulse rifle and a few other things we wouldn't want to try to get through Customs."

I grinned but didn't ask what he was keeping there. "Rabbit, can you slice the schematics and plans for the Promenade maintenance spaces?"

"Really, Zack?" His face had that look he uses when someone asks a stupid question, or at least what he considers a stupid question. "I updated those as soon as we logged into the local net. Downloading to your links now." He turned to Wells. "Yours is encrypted, military protocol. I could slice it, but it might be unpleasant. I need your permission for access to loop you into our coms."

Wells only hesitated for a second, then nodded. My own link pinged as Wells was added to the com network. Cleo and Grace rose, a decision apparently having been reached.

"Come on, Eddie," she said, using her pet name for Rabbit. "Let's go shopping. We'll meet these boys at the Apollo in a few hours."

We kitted up near Deuce's locker and made our way to the freight entrance to the Promenade. Rabbit had updated our fake identity chits and created one for Wells. We were whisked up the dropshaft to the maintenance level just below the wide walkway across the arch. Above, the hotels and spires of the entertainment venues reached up almost a hundred meters to the very apex of the Tycho dome.

We made our way through the access and maintenance tunnels until we were under the Dai Ichi. I sent Deuce up to the service entrance on the near side of the lobby while Wells and I continued on to the far side. Deuce signaled when he was at the top of the access shaft, and I had him hold position until we reached the other side of the broad lobby. Once we reached the top of our access shaft, I gave the go-ahead.

Wells and I stepped out of a maintenance hatch behind a false wall near the dropshafts. Across from the shafts, the main desk area and AI kiosks were quietly busy with morning checking in and out. I motioned left and Wells headed that way. He moved like a professional, eyes on a swivel but not obviously checking anything. To any but the most astute observer, he was a maintenance man unhurriedly moving to his next task. I approved.

I made my own way around the lobby, checking sightlines and potential blind spots. I had to admit, the lobby made a good site for a meeting, at least from the kidnapper's point of view. It was broad and open with few places for concealment or monitoring. Any watchers would have to blend in with a shifting crowd of people. Anyone staying in one place or circling the area would stand out. The overhead was high but wasn't an open atrium with floors or rooms looking down, so overwatch would have to be electronic. I passed Deuce making his own circuit and met up with Wells on the other side from where we started. We reentered the access shaft and dropped down to the service deck.

Wells stopped me as soon as we stepped out of the shaft. "Hang on, Mbele," he said in a low growl. "What the hell was this all about? There's no way we can set up any surveillance on that lobby without being marked in a hot minute. If these operators are as good as you claim, they'll either abort or flood the space with numbers, especially since they don't need to care about being covert,"

"You're right." My respect for Wells jumped up another notch. "This was a dry run for the meeting. I want them to see me and Deuce as well as you and Cleo. They'll expect us to make the effort, and Zameda won't be happy unless you're present somehow. What he doesn't get is that no matter how good Rabbit's monitoring is, he won't get anything but static from the man we're really meeting here."

"And who might that be?" Wells sounded skeptical. "Some sort of hot shit black ops operator?"

I looked him over carefully, trying to decide whether to read him in completely or not. "Something like that."

He sighed. "Look, Mbele, two days ago, if anyone had talked to me about Revenants hiding out in the Belt and infiltrating government agencies, I'd have labeled them a paranoid nutcase. Now I'm not sure who I can trust. But I for sure am not backing you in a potential ambush situation without knowing who the hell is behind all this."

"How did you get hooked up with Zameda in the first

place?" I asked.

He frowned. "You're not answering my question."

"I will," I said. "Humor me."

He folded his arms and drew back a half step, glaring. I thought for a second he was going to turn and walk away, but he seemed to come to some sort of decision. "I was in the Provost Guard during the war and Pacification. I spent a lot of time on Mars tracking down guys like you. Some of Metternich's old supporters had false IDs and legends in place, so tracking them down was a 'challenge' as my old CO used to call it. Anyway, once Mars was declared 'reintegrated,' the military drawdown left me out of a job. The FBS was hiring, and it seemed a good fit."

"And then you got posted to Highpoint." I said with a nod.

"Not right away. I was stationed on Mars at first, sort of a lateral move. Spent the first year running down smugglers and war profiteers, even ran a few operations against outfits like the Red Dragons. Got transferred to Gagarin Center for eighteen months, same mission, before being offered a staff job on Earth. I took it, thinking I was building a career." He smiled wryly. "But at Central, it's not about how good you are, it's all who you know and where you come from. I was born in East Podunk Iowa. No family or money or powerful friends to push me forward. I ended up as a glorified clerk writing reports on other people's investigations."

"And then you made a mistake."

"Oh, yeah." He gave a harsh laugh and rubbed the back of his neck. "It seems my superiors didn't want an analysis of the investigations I was reviewing, only summaries they could pass up the line to make it look like they were working hard. When I pointed out a pattern that indicated graft, or at least violations of confidentiality, I was dead-ended to an office in Tierra del Fuego writing prisoner transfer requests for the supermax prison in Antarctica."

"Ouch," I winced.

"I bitched and moaned and sent in a dozen requests for transfer," Wells continued. "Then there was some sort of shake-up in my previous chain of command. A new supervisor wanted me even farther away than Antarctica and cut me orders for Highpoint. That was almost two years ago."

Wells stopped and looked me in the eye. "Why do you want to know all this? What's my life story to you or to this op?"

"You like working for Zameda?" I asked, holding his eye.

"No," he said, his tone still belligerent. "He's a prig and a bastard, but he's reasonably honest and competent. This is his big operational tour before he moves into the command suite down Earthside. He needs one big score to cinch a position on the Director's staff and from there move into politics."

I thought for a moment more then came to a decision. "Thank you for all that. Now listen. I'm going to read you in on the whole story as I know it. Close hold, even from Zameda. You good with that?" He didn't pause more than a heartbeat before nodding. "The guys we're up against are what's left of the First Covert Operations Battalion, Metternich's Own. Most died in the war or were rounded up by you and your mates. Some, the most senior or hard-core, had escape plans and legends in place and escaped."

"Like Corwin," Wells said.

"Like Corwin," I agreed. "Though I suspect he may have been a sleeper, placed before the war. In any event, the survivors hooked up out in the Belt and soon took over the smuggling and protection rackets there. Last few years, though, they've gotten leadership and rediscovered purpose."

"Wait," Wells interrupted. "You said these guys are what's left of the First. I've brought some of them in, killed others who wouldn't surrender. They were absolute fanatics, loyal to nothing or no one but Metternich himself. Who could take over and lead them?"

I looked him in the eye and made sure he held mine. "Metternich is still alive. He's the man Deuce and I are meeting later today."

"Bullshit!" said Wells. "Metternich was killed when Tharsis Government House was bombed during the war."

"That's the official line," I agreed. "But he was always a slippery bastard. He got out. For a while, he became Henry Middleton, a mid-level enforcer, who rose to run security for Colin Jones and the Red Dragons. That ended almost a year ago when Jones was shot by his own men. I've talked to him myself at least twice since then."

"Middleton." Wells rubbed the back of his neck again. "That makes a weird sort of sense. He came out of nowhere but shut down some of our best leads into the Dragons. This is *Honto?* He's really alive?"

I nodded. "And I have no doubt he's behind this play with Deuce's daughter." I left it at that, giving Wells time to mull it over."

We hooked up with Deuce and made our way to the Apollo after switching out to civilian clothes. No one spoke. We'd all seen the meeting area and recognized the impossibility of stealth coverage. Any overwatch would depend on Rabbit's ability to slice the security system and follow us with our links. We'd position Wells and Cleo somewhere in the lobby, but they'd be marked by Metternich's people and not much help if everything went sideways.

I doubted the Colonel would try anything. He went to

a lot of trouble to arrange this meeting. He needed us for something. The betrayal would come later, after he had what he wanted.

Chapter 19

"Honey, we're home," Deuce called as he palmed the lock to the suite of rooms Cleo had secured.

We followed him in. Rabbit sat in his chair facing the door and Grace stood behind him, one hand on his shoulder. I knew right away something was wrong.

"It wasn't my fault, Zack," Rabbit babbled. "I tried to stop her. I told her you'd be mad, but you know how she gets. She just took her needler and batons and left. Didn't say where she was going, when she'd be back, nothing."

"Slow down, Rabbit," I said. "Who?" But the sinking sensation in my chest told me who.

"Cleo. She left just after we checked in." Rabbit flinched when he looked at my face. "I told her not to go, but she didn't listen."

I struggled to keep my face blank, my voice neutral. "Slowly, tell me what happened. Did you meet or see anyone at the shops or in the passages here?"

"No, Zack." Rabbit shook his head so hard I thought his teeth would rattle. "We were clean. Cleo took point and I watched our tail. No one followed or noticed us. We got here and she had already booked the suite through her link. The AI at the desk took cash without a blip. This is that kind of place, I guess. Just as we got into the room, Cleo got a ping from her link. It was encrypted and I didn't hear what was said. She just listened for a few seconds, then grabbed her weapons and left."

"Did you call her link?"

Rabbit nodded. "She's turned it off."

Shit! This isn't the time for Cleo to go off on her own. I thought we were done with this crap. I felt a pang in my guts. This was too much like what happened before our divorce. "Can you track it, like you did on Mars?"

"Maybe, from the ship. I don't have the right setup here and I'd have had to lock onto her before she shut the link down to be sure."

"Never mind." I growled. "Damn! We don't have time for this shit. We only have an hour before the meeting."

I felt the old familiar pain in my chest. *After all we've done, all we've said, she's left me again.* When it came to Cleopatra Lee, if heartaches were *yuan,* I'd be the richest fool alive. I shook my head. *Enough! Deuce needs me. Time to warrior up and continue the mission.*

"Where's Zameda?" I asked.

"He's at the FBS station. He wants to hear from you ASAP." Rabbit smirked. "He's mad because he can't get a fix on us. My scrambler protocols are better than the FBS's. We can talk to him, but he can't track us."

I took a moment's satisfaction in that. "Ok, tie him into our coms, full access."

Rabbit frowned but didn't protest. Maybe he was mellowing.

"Mbele, where the hell are you?" Zameda demanded before I could say anything. "I made it clear I was to oversee every phase of this operation. Don't think you can cut me out without consequences."

I didn't suggest that he perform an anatomic impossibility on himself, not immediately anyway. I actually considered what cards he held here. It came down to the money. He had no legal hold over us, only a financial one. The flimsy conspiracy allegation he'd used to freeze our assets wouldn't hold up in any court outside of Highpoint, even if it would take weeks, maybe months, to get the case in front of a Federal Magistrate. If Cleo had been at my side, I might have cared. She would have cared. But Cleo wasn't here. She was off God knew where once again, and I was in this alone.

"Eat shit and die, Zameda," I said. "I told you before, you have my money but that's all. And I no longer give a damn about the money. I've been broke before. It ain't the end of the universe." I made a slashing motion toward Rabbit, and he cut the connection.

"Any chance he can trace us, Rabbit?

"Seriously, Zack?" He snorted. "Give me a little credit."

I pointed to Wells. "What about him? His link is military spec. It's trackable."

"I disabled it as soon as he gave me permission for access. He can talk to us, but that's all." Wells shot him a hard look, but Rabbit just shrugged. "Operational security."

"Decision time, Wells," I said. "You can go back to Zameda at the local FBS station, but we'll be gone and neither you nor he will find us before we finish this. Or, you can tag along, maybe even help, but without Zameda or the FBS knowing where you are or what you're doing."

"What about the Pathists?" Wells asked. "I know the girl is your top priority, I get it. She's your partner's daughter, family. But the Path is a real threat. The attack at Highpoint proved that."

"I have my own reasons for going after the Fourfold

Path." My voice was flat but left no doubt. "I gave my word to a friend that I'd take them down. That's got nothing to do with Zameda and his game."

"My last orders were to stay with you when you meet the kidnappers and report my observations. Those orders haven't changed, whether or not I'm in communication with Zameda. I'll stay." Wells paused and grinned. "Besides, it'll be fun to stick it to that self-righteous prig."

"All right, then," I said. I didn't fully trust Wells, but I did expect he'd be professional. "Without Cleo, we can't cover both sides of the lobby. We'll be counting on you, Rabbit, to give us overwatch and alert me or Wells to any unexpected company."

"Will do, Zack. I've sliced into both the Dai Ichi and TychoNet security cams for a hundred meters in all directions. That should give you enough warning if the Colonel tries anything clever."

"Wells, I'll need you to hold the maintenance shaft we used earlier. That's our exfil if we need to abort or the meeting goes sideways. Rabbit should be able to slice the alarms to let you get through with full kit and a couple of flash-bangs if we need to make a quick exit."

He nodded. "What's our approach?"

"Deuce and I will go in openly through the public lifts and main lobby entrance. It will limit our weapons and armor." I turned to Deuce. "Blades and augment vests are the only things we'll be able to get past Promenade security screening. No pulse rifle, partner."

Deuce grinned. "As long as the Colonel's guys play by the same rules, it won't be a problem." He paused. "Sure would help to have Cleo along, though."

I frowned and pushed down the sudden flare of anger. *Damn her.* Cleo's unarmed skills might be the difference between success and failure if it came to a fight. "Can't worry about that now, Deuce." I turned to

Wells. "You'll retrace our route from today. I'll need you at the maintenance hatch by 18:00. Rabbit will coordinate coms and routes."

"Not sure I like having only one exfil option," he said. "Any other routes, Conejo?"

Rabbit looked startled at being addressed directly but recovered quickly after a glance at me. "Not unless you want to shoot your way out through the public lobby. But once you get through the hatch, I can route you at least three different ways to the dropshafts."

"It'll have to do." Wells sighed. "When to we leave?"

I checked my link. "It's 15:30 now. Everyone get some rest and something to eat. We'll dress out and be ready to leave at 17:15."

"I'm coming with you," Grace spoke up for the first time since we'd returned from the recon.

"The hell you are," said Deuce, his voice rising. "I can't risk you bein' taken, too."

She put her hand on his arm and looked at his face in that weird way she 'saw' with her implants. "I need to know that Ingrid is all right, Sven. I need to go to her."

"No!" Deuce was almost shouting now. "I can't let you give yourself up to the Colonel. What if he decides to settle your debt by slittin' your throat? I can't lose both of you."

"He won't do that," said Grace calmly. "He needs both of us alive until you've done the job he has for you. Ingrid needs me. She must be terrified. I can keep her calm and safe until you and Zack can get us back."

Her tone contained no doubt that we would be able to do exactly that. An idea started to take shape in my mind at that moment. *Maybe we can make this work for us.*

"You may be onto something, Grace," I said, ignoring the angry look Deuce flashed at me. "Rabbit, can you rig some way to track Grace without her link? Something like the Zylene tracer we used at Highpoint?"

Rabbit thought for a second. “Not here. The sensor net isn’t tuned to pick up small trace leaks. Lunar gravity is low, but no one will float away if the grid fails.”

“Trace her link?” I asked.

“Maybe, but it’s vulnerable to any high-end privacy jammer.”

Deuce took her hands, his head bowed. “Please, Grace. I’m beggin’ you. Don’t do this.”

Grace reached up and touched his cheek. In that instant, I saw Rabbit’s face light up. “I know how we can track Grace wherever she goes,” he said smugly. I held out my hand, inviting him to continue.

“Her pendant and implants,” he said as if it were obvious to anyone. When we all looked puzzled, he continued. “Her pendant sends a signal to the implants with an encryption of some sort. It must be a unique frequency or blocked encryption, otherwise she’d get all sorts of random inputs from other links, com signals, even the broadcast adverts from every store she passes.”

Grace nodded in affirmation. “I don’t understand how it works, but the tech who tuned my pendant said it used some sort of code that canceled out interference from other sources.”

“And you can track that?” I asked.

“Not track, exactly,” Rabbit answered rubbing his chin. “But maybe ping it and get a response. It won’t be the same as continuous monitoring, and the range will be short, but it should let us find Grace wherever they take her.”

“Get on it,” I said. “Let me know when you’re ready, and we’ll test it here before we leave.”

Deuce pulled away from Gace and spun to face me, fists clenched, eyes hard. “You can’t be serious, LT. I can’t let you do this.”

I held up both hands, palms out, as Grace reached

out and took Deuce's arm again. He stiffened but didn't pull away.

"Think, Deuce," I said as calmly as I could. "If we don't know where they're holding Ingrid, we're at the Colonel's mercy. He can force us to do anything he wants as long as he can hold her over you. If we track Grace to her, we can figure out how to get them both out. Then we can take the Colonel down once and for all."

Deuce looked like he was going to object, but Grace spoke before he could. "Zack is right, Sven. If anyone can get us out, you can. It's our only chance to end this."

Deuce seemed to deflate and nodded once before turning away from us both. I hoped Grace's faith in us wasn't misplaced.

Chapter 20

We gathered in the common room of the suite a little before 17:15. Deuce and I were in dark business suits of real cashmere, each of which cost as much as the average ice miner made in a year. They fit perfectly. Cleo had gone all out and had exquisite taste. *Damn her! Just when things had begun to look good for us, she'd sabotaged it again.*

Deuce didn't look comfortable, but he did look fashionable. Grace wore a shimmering evening gown that both contrasted with, and complemented Deuce's get-up as she took his arm.

Wells on the other hand looked deadly, dressed in black body armor and tactical vest with a pair of Huang needlers in cross draw shoulder holsters and two flash-bang grenades at his belt.

"Are you ready to test the tracer?" asked Rabbit, a little tentatively.

"You sound concerned, Edward," said Grace. "Is there a problem?"

"No, I mean, not a serious one." He looked even more uncomfortable. "The tracer sends out an interrogation signal that your implants will respond to. It's part of the calibration function. But to be useful at a distance, it needs to be fairly strong. It may interrupt your pendant's input. It will be very short, but ... It might be unpleasant."

"How unpleasant?" Deuce demanded. "Could it hurt her?"

"We won't know until we try it, Sven," said Grace. "Go ahead, Edward."

Rabbit brushed a key, and Grace closed her eyes and winced. She took a deep breath and said, "That was interesting. Not painful, but definitely not pleasant."

"It should be less intense as you get farther away," said Rabbit, "The range is a bit limited though, no more than 1500 meters. I've given Zack a pinger that will relay the response back here to me. Hopefully they won't take you out of range too quickly."

We sent Wells out first, tracking him through his link. Once he reached the maintenance dropshaft, Rabbit sliced the security screen and got him inside. It would take him a while to make his way across the Promenade to the Dai Ichi.

We took a limo to the central lifts, right below the Dai Ichi. We were dressed the part, and a flash of cash got us past the security detail. Grace and Deuce attracted attention on the lift and as we strolled down the Promenade toward the hotel, Deuce because of his size and Grace for the air of understated elegance that made her such a compelling performer. I trailed behind, playing the part of Deuce's wingman, or perhaps Grace's bodyguard.

Around us swirled exquisitely dressed men and women, seeing and being seen, looking like a bouquet of hothouse flowers. The Promenade ran across the entire arc of the main dome, nearly five kilometers. Over a hundred meters wide and sheathed in transparent duroplast, it elevated the rich and famous high above the swirling masses of Armstrong Boulevard and the surrounding streets and alleys. Elite hotels, restaurants, and clubs lined the Lunar north side, leaving the opposite wall open to look out over Tycho City through the dome to the floor of Tycho Crater and its magnificent Earthrise.

We approached the hotel lobby, drawing hardly a glance from a liveried doorman who clearly doubled as security. The space was wide and tall, but much of the height was an illusion created by clever VR screens and forced perspective. Across from the main entrance was the front desk and the concierge office. To the right was Panache, the four-star restaurant that catered to both guests and passing celebrities. To the left was a comfortable seating area with bar service and discreet banquette for private meetings.

I immediately marked two operators, one on each end of the lobby, standing still, not even trying to blend in. "What have you got, Rabbit?" I asked subvocally through my link as we crossed the lobby.

"Two ahead of you, one behind. Not picking out anyone else, at least no one carrying weapons."

"I've got the two at either end of the lobby," I answered. "Who's the third?"

"At the bar, third from the end, green jacket," said Rabbit. "He's got a Huang pneumatic under his left armpit."

I glanced right and saw him. "Not sure," I said. "We'll mark him, but he may just be off-duty private security. Is Wells in position?"

"He's there."

"Here," said Wells in my link. "I can hear you both."

"Good," I said. "I need you to hold that maintenance hatch, it's our exfil if this goes wrong."

"Will do. Just keep me in the link. No surprises."

"We're starting across the lobby now," I said. "Rabbit, any other players?"

"No, and that's odd. I'd expect the Colonel to flood the room with a show of force. I've linked Wells into my feed just in case anything changes."

"Link is clear and stable," said Wells. "I see the Tango at the bar, looks like he's separate from the guards."

We crossed the open lobby, angling left toward the private area. The two operators we'd marked paced us, arriving at the cluster of seats at the same time we approached. The guy at the bar didn't move, didn't seem to notice us.

I stepped in close, getting into their personal space without actually touching either man. They both stared straight ahead, like soldiers at attention, holding their positions just long enough to show they weren't intimidated. They took a step back and turned, admitting us to the space and into the presence of the man who sat at the nearest banquette.

His face had changed again, narrower with high cheekbones and a thin, slightly hooked nose. His prominent chin sported a neatly trimmed goatee, along with a narrow moustache above a prominent upper lip. The eyes were green now but held the same cold certainty that had haunted my dreams since my time in the Bear. No matter how he changed his appearance, the eyes stayed the same. I slid into the bench seat across from him and held his gaze despite the fluttering in my gut.

Grace slid into the seat next to me and Deuce remained standing, one hand on her shoulder. He glared down at the man on the other side of the banquette.

"Welcome, First Sergeant," said Colonel Metternich. He turned to Grace. "And you brought the lovely Ms. Tyler."

"You're the one who called this meeting, Colonel," I said. "What do you want us to do?"

He chuckled. "Direct as always, Zachariah. No comments on my new face?" I didn't answer, just stared at him. I didn't trust my voice not to break.

Grace broke the silence. "Please, sir, I need to see my daughter."

Metternich smiled and slid a small holoprojector across the table. It activated and showed a wide shot of a comfortable room. A child sat on the floor playing a puzzle game on another projector. A middle-aged woman sat on the arm of a nearby chair watching her.

"She can't see that, asshole," Deuce growled.

"Oh, yes. Sometimes I forget." He reached out and turned on the sound. A child's voice singing a nursery rhyme filled the space above the table.

"Ingrid!" Grace leaned forward cupping her hands around the hologram, her voice almost a sob.

The little girl's head came up. "Mommy?"

Before Grace could respond, Metternich clicked off the holo. "I trust that is sufficient proof of life for all of you."

Deuce's hands came up as if to reach across the table. The men behind him drew blackened-finish needlers from shoulder holsters with a speed that confirmed their SpecOps background. I held up both hands.

"Deuce, stand down." I looked to each of the men in turn before adding, "No threat here, gentlemen." At a slight nod from Metternich, they holstered their weapons and stepped back.

Metternich looked up at Deuce, not intimidated by his size and anger. "I understand your concern, First Sergeant. You obviously care about your daughter. She is quite safe for the time being, under the care of a professional nurse. She is warm and dry and has plenty to eat and enough entertainment to divert her young mind. For now."

"Take me to her," said Grace. Her voice didn't break. Her tone was quiet but brooked no denial. For a brief moment, the Colonel looked nonplussed.

"What do you want from us?" I asked before he could answer Grace.

"I need you to recover something that was stolen from me. And eliminate the people who took it."

"We're not assassins," I said. "Do your own dirty work."

Metternich laughed. "Of course you're not. Your body count is just a function of bad karma. Tell yourself whatever lies you need to, Zachariah. I don't care. I do care about recovering my property and eliminating the Fourfold Path."

That stopped me. *The Fourfold Path? What the hell?* "What does the Path have to do with this?"

Metternich smiled. "They have everything to do with it, Zachariah. They stole a datastick containing the genetic codes for the regulator genes controlling the p324 neuroreceptor. Then they eliminated the only three men in the Ulan Bator delegation on Highpoint who could have reconstructed the codes from memory."

I cocked my head, puzzled. I wasn't sure what the p324 receptor was or why he cared when it hit me. *The embryos we'd stolen for Kwai Chang Wu. They must have this protein, and it must be the one that would allow them to accept a stable nanofiber bond. They were cloned at a lab in UB, the same one that was building the LaGrange point station. The same one that Kwai Hong owned controlling interest in.*

"The *Federales* still have those embryos of yours, don't they," I asked. "What's to keep them from discovering the codes and using them?"

"They can if they know where to look," Metternich said with an approving nod. "They may even realize that the cloned embryos have a single gene variant found in only one person in ten thousand, but they won't know what they're looking at or why it's significant. And I can't exactly ask them to give me the genome map for the embryos."

"What about the lab in UB? They made the clones; don't they know why this p324 receptor is important?"

"Again, the men who might know were all killed in the attack on Highpoint," Metternich replied. "So you see, the only record of the codes is on that datastick."

"Bullshit. Ingrid was taken before the attack," I said. "You planned to have us go after those codes before the Ulan Bator delegation even got to Highpoint."

Metternich gave a small shrug. "My relationship with Ulan Bator has not been one of mutual trust. And the Fourfold Path is fanatically opposed to the type of cloning those codes represent. I knew they had the data, but the attack on the delegation caught us by surprise."

"So send the crack team who kidnapped Ingrid to get it back. Why us?"

"My people are at a disadvantage here in Tycho," said Metternich. "You have contacts and deep local roots that we can't match. I could kick down enough doors to find the codes, but it would take time, and time is of the essence. Besides, my forces are committed elsewhere."

"We'll do it." Deuce interrupted before I could process what the Colonel might mean by time being important. "Whatever it takes to get Ingrid back."

I glared up at him, but he wasn't looking at me. He only had eyes for Grace as she held the holoprojector as if it were a precious gem. "We'll get her back," he said.

"Take me to her," Grace said, looking directly at Metternich.

"Of course." But his eyes were on Deuce, not Grace. Deuce nodded and stepped back. Metternich motioned to one of the bodyguards who stepped close and ran the wand of a signal scanner over Grace.

"She's clean," the man said. "Her link is deactivated."

"Thank you, Isaac," said Metternich. He held Deuce's eye. "If we detect any signal from her link or from a concealed tracker, I won't hesitate to have them both killed."

"And if either of them is harmed, I'll rip your lungs out through your rectum," growled Deuce.

"Colorful," Metternich chuckled. "For both our sakes, you had better succeed."

Isaac came forward again and touched Grace on the shoulder. She rose, squeezing Deuce's hand as she did. I felt him tense, but he didn't move.

"Do your job, then come get us," she told him.

Through my link, I pinged her implant and got a solid return. She closed her eyes for a second and cocked her head slightly. No one noticed. More importantly, Isaac's scanner didn't chirp.

"How soon do you need results, Colonel?" I asked. "You said time was short."

"Forty-eight hours, maybe," he said. "No more than seventy-two hours. I can stall the Mongolians for that long, but I need those codes if our arrangement is to move forward."

"Arrange..." Then it hit me. "The UB LaGrange station. You're behind that."

"We provided much of the seed money needed for the construction, money that has already been spent." Metternich said. He passed a hand across the face that wasn't his real face, and I realized how old and tired he looked. "In return they were to create a new set of clones. But if I don't have the codes by the time the Federation grants them the license to incorporate a new LaGrange habitat, the deal is off, and I'm left with nothing."

Much as I wanted to tell the Colonel to pound sand and walk out, I knew he held all the cards. This was why he'd taken Ingrid. I would never help him voluntarily. Instead, I asked, "What else? Do you have any idea where the Path is based?"

"Only that they are here in Tycho City. Relatively recently arrived after fleeing Earth. We know they're here but little more than that. The assault on the delegation at Highpoint was a surprise, possibly intended to disrupt the plans for the new habitat." Metternich looked me in the eye. "It's a shame one of the attackers could not have been taken alive."

We were in a firefight and the bad guys had no intention of surrendering, and you know it. But I said nothing, keeping the thought to myself.

The Colonel sighed. "It's air out the lock now." He slid a data stick across the small table. "This is all we have on their recent activity and possible contacts here in Tycho. Contact information once you have the codes is also there."

I scooped up the tiny stick and turned to go without a second look. Deuce stood staring down at Metternich, fists clenched, his eyes cold as moonrock.

"Stand down, Deuce," I said softly. "Mission first." I felt him ease a bit as he turned and followed me.

"What's happening, Mbele?" said Wells through my link. "I only got your side of the meeting; the rest was just static."

"He's wearing a personal scrambler," Rabbit piped up. "Best I've ever seen. I'll try to clean it up, but there's not much there."

"No surprise there," I said. "Wells, head on out. We won't need exfil. Meet back at the dropshaft." I nodded to Deuce's inquiring look. "Tracking is working. She's still in range. Rabbit will find her."

Chapter 21

We left the Dai Ichi, but loitered on the Promenade as Rabbit tracked the pings from Grace's implant.

"Which way Rabbit?" I asked.

"Stay around the Dai Ichi," said Rabbit. "She's pinging right on top of you. Is she still in the lobby?"

"No, one of Metternich's guys led her away. She's not in our sight line."

Rabbit didn't answer right away. I was about to repeat myself when he spoke again, excited. "She's gone vertical. She's about 90 meters above and 20 meters left of your position."

She's in a hotel room. They're keeping Ingrid right here. "We're coming back, Rabbit."

"But what if they move Grace somewhere else?" he asked.

I thought about the room where Ingrid was playing. It had the look of a high-end suite in a hotel. "They won't. This is their home base, hiding in plain sight."

We picked up Wells at the dropshaft and caught a

public transit capsule back to the Apollo. As we settled into the bench seats, Deuce up front, Wells and me in the back, Wells leaned close to speak in my ear.

"What the hell was that about, Mbele?" he asked. "You want me to believe that was Metternich back there?"

"Believe what you want. I know the Colonel. I dream about him most nights; it was him."

Wells grunted. "I'll have to take your word on that. All I got over the link whenever he spoke was static. I gathered that he had a task for you lot, something about codes and the Path."

I filled him in on the Colonel's side of the conversation including the significance of the genetic codes. At first, he scoffed. Then, after a quick demonstration of my own nano-augmented speed he sat quietly for a long minute.

"Holy shit," he whispered. "He wants to breed a race of superhumans." He paused. "But how does he plan to raise the clones? This will take generations."

"I imagine he's got the infrastructure somewhere out in the Belt. He and his Revenants have been taking over operations out there ever since the War." I pondered his point for a moment. "It wouldn't be that hard. Children are precious to most Belter families. No lack of fosters, especially if there's a little extra money in it."

Wells only grunted at that, and we completed the ride back to the Apollo in silence. We exited the capsule a hundred meters from the hotel and ran a quick surveillance detection drill. Several random turns and trips down side alleys later, we entered the lobby.

The third operator from the Dai Ichi sat in a side chair near the dropshafts scanning a filmbook, pointedly ignoring us. He'd changed his green jacket for a dark gray jumpsuit and wore a link interface skullcap. He looked like an off-duty pilot enjoying a rest cycle before his next transit, but I recognized him. Deuce did, too, and glanced at me as if to say, *What's the play?*

I gave him a hand signal to stand down. I didn't know who this guy was but, so far, he hadn't made a move on us. For all we knew, he was working for the Colonel, keeping tabs on our progress. If Wells made the man, he gave no sign of it. We passed him and entered the dropshaft.

"The third operator was in the lobby," said Wells as we started up, his eyes straight ahead, tone flat. I smiled. The man was good.

"We noticed." We hit our floor and stepped out into a small lobby. Deuce dropped into a fighting stance and drew back his right arm. I stepped to the side to give Wells a clear field of fire as my nanos sprang to life, augmenting speed and strength. Wells didn't miss a beat as he drew one of his Huangs, assuming a shooter's stance.

The giant facing us across the small space didn't move. Maybe his right eyelid twitched, maybe not. He ignored Deuce, looked Wells up and down, then focused on me.

"You, I know," he said. "You want fight again?"

"Stand down, Deuce, Zack." Cleo stepped out from behind the giant's shoulder. "Uncle Po, no fight."

The giant snorted and turned his back on us and walked away down the passageway toward our rooms.

"Rabbit won't open the door," said Cleo. "You need to tell him it's ok to let us in."

"Is it?" I asked. "Where the hell have you been, Cleo. You don't get to walk out on us just before a critical operation and then walk back in again like nothing happened. I thought you and I were past this kind of bullshit."

Cleo took a half step forward, her eyes hard. I'd seen that look before, but this time I wasn't backing down. I held her angry gaze as I stepped forward into her space. She faltered, looked away and stepped back.

"You want to explain yourself?"

She looked up at me with those hard eyes but, after a second, they softened, and she sighed.

"While you and Deuce were checking out the Dai Ichi, Uncle Po found me. He needed to see me right away and so I went out to meet him. He knows where to find the Pathists who ordered the attack at the Planitia."

I held up my hand. "Wait. Uncle Po 'found you'? How?"

She looked away. "He had my com locus." I opened my mouth, but she went on in a rush. "I tagged it to our business locus before shutting it down. I only meant to check through the business site every day to see if we had any inquiries. We can't afford to be out of commission for very long, and as long as Zameda has our accounts frozen I thought we could pick up some off-books jobs. Uncle Po found the business locus and left a message."

"And you responded? How could you do something that stupid? We need to be invisible here, at least until we get Ingrid and Grace back." As soon as I said it, I realized I shouldn't have mentioned Grace.

Cleo jerked as if I'd struck her. "Grace? What's happened to Grace?"

"She's at the Dai Ichi, with Ingrid. Which you'd know if you'd been with us."

She looked around as if there were others in earshot. "Please, Zack, we need to get into the suite and talk. Uncle Po has important information about the Path. You need to hear him out."

The mention of the Pathists stopped my angry tirade for the moment. I pinged Rabbit through my link. "Open up, Rabbit, we're coming in."

Several minutes later, we were gathered in the sitting area of the two-room suite. Sitting area was the hotel's term for the two by three-meter space between the two bedrooms. Cleo and I sat opposite each other in the two chairs, while Wells stood leaning against the doorframe of the right-hand bedroom. Rabbit was set up with his gear at the small table directly across from the entrance. Deuce and Uncle Po carefully avoided each other's space, like two predators staking out territory.

"What have you got to say, Cleo?" I asked. "We needed you for the meeting with the Colonel."

"What do they want, Zack? Why did they take Ingrid and Grace?"

I looked past her to Po standing near the wall, motionless as a rock. "What does he know about the Path? Because the price for Ingrid and Grace is the leaders of the Fourfold Path. They're here on the Moon and the Colonel wants us to take them out. So if your 'Uncle' knows something, we need to know too."

Cleo turned and said something to Po in a language I didn't understand. He answered in the same language, making slight gestures toward me and Deuce.

"Po knows where they are," said Cleo, turning back to me. "But they're well protected. He doesn't think you have enough firepower."

I cocked my head at Deuce who shrugged. Wells shook his head. "We're too thin for any kind of serious firefight," he said. I was surprised but gratified that he said 'we.'

"What about Zameda?" I asked. "We can tip him off and let his people do the heavy lifting."

Wells grimaced. "By the time the FBS gets their act together, someone will have tipped the bastards off and they'll be long gone."

Po seemed to have understood us and nodded. "Time is short," he said. "Only here for a day. Move now."

I was about to ask how he knew that when there was a pounding at the door.

"Zack Mbele," a loud voice I recognized shouted. "Open up! We need to talk."

I made a calming motion toward Po and Cleo went to

his side, speaking softly. I opened the door a crack and looked out into the passageway.

"Hey, Hank," I said. "How's it hanging?"

Henri 'Hank' Boucher stood in the corridor with a short, dark-haired man in a Lunar Security Sergeant's uniform. I recognized him as the mystery operator who'd been at the Dai Ichi and in the lobby here.

"May we come in?" asked Boucher. I noticed he now wore Lieutenant's bars on his collar.

"Congratulations on the promotion, Hank." I stood in the doorway, continuing to block it. "How did you find us?"

He laughed. "Did you really think Conejo's trick with the transponder would hold once you left the ship? Facial recognition AI picked you up as soon as you entered the spaceport. I got flagged, and yes, I'm keeping tabs on you. We tracked you here. When you and Deuce ran your recon on the Dai Ichi, I got curious and put a man in the lobby." He hooked a thumb at the Sergeant. "This is Sergeant Manny Carillo, by the way. He's former Special Forces as well, like you and Deuce."

I cocked my head. "Carillo? Second Battalion out of Planitia?"

"Aye, LT." He grinned. "Bravo Team. We ran that Op against the Mac Tir with your boys just after the Colonel took power. Good to see you're still alive."

"So, Zack," said Boucher, his voice less friendly than before. "You want to tell me who you were meeting at the Dai Ichi, or should we go down to HQ and talk?"

I doubted he had probable cause to detain us, but you couldn't be too sure these days. I opened the door and stepped back. "You better come in."

Hank took in the crowd in the small room. He nodded to Cleo and Deuce, looked hard at Po for a second and then saw Wells. He shook his head. "Your Boss is very upset with you, Agent Wells. Been burning up the coms trying to find you."

Wells smiled wryly. "He's the one who told me to stay close to Mbele."

"About that, Hank," I said. "How could you track us when Zameda can't?"

"The FBS doesn't have their own surveillance assets in Tycho. We have an agreement to share with them." He paused and looked around. "I have a lot of discretion about what gets shared. I saw the freeze he placed on your accounts and got curious. What's he got on you?"

I silently checked with Cleo, who cocked her head and nodded. "Zameda accused us of having something to do with the attack on the Ulan Bator trade group on Highpoint a couple of days ago. He froze our accounts to try to force us to lead him to the Fourfold Pathists who ordered the attack."

"Why would Zameda think you had anything to do with the Path?"

"Because Cleo used to work for them back before the FBS broke them up a few years ago. Her Uncle Po here," I gestured to the grim giant. "Was her trainer and handler. When the original heads of the Fourfold Path were captured, Cleo saw her chance at freedom and took it."

"We heard the Path had made a comeback, but nobody expected them to be able to pull off an operation like Highpoint," said Hank. "Is Zameda right? Has the new leadership tried to recruit Cleo?"

"No," Cleo answered. "Uncle Po broke with them before the raids ten years ago. He spent time in Antarctica on a smuggling charge, but there was never enough evidence to tie him directly to the hard-core Pathists. When he got out and heard the Path had reconstituted itself, he went looking for me to try to protect me." She touched my arm.

"Sorry I didn't tell you sooner, Zack, but Uncle Po only explained it when we met here."

"What's this got to do with your meeting at the Dai Ichi?" Hank asked.

"That's what started all this in the first place." I moved closer to Deuce. "Ok to fill Hank in, partner?" He nodded, and I turned back to Boucher. "A bunch of ex-Black Ops operators from the old Third Directorate kidnapped Deuce's daughter. They're holding her and her mother to force us to do a job for them. We were at the Planitia Club to meet a contact from the kidnappers when the attack went down. That's why Zameda thinks we're involved."

To Hank's credit, he only blinked a couple of times at the news that Deuce had a daughter. "What sort of job?" was all he asked.

I laughed. "You're not gonna believe it, but they want us to take out the Pathists, same as Zameda. Different reasons, same job. Po here knows where they're holed up, but they're well protected. We don't have the juice to take them down alone." I paused and looked Hank in the eye. "How'd you like to make Captain?"

Chapter 22

It didn't take much to sell Hank on the idea of raiding the Pathists' base. The harder sell was letting us go along. Hank tried to stand on principle. We weren't law enforcement officers and couldn't participate in an armed raid by his Tactical Unit. I pointed out that we had a vested interest in taking the Pathists down, and he knew very well that we could handle ourselves. Besides, Wells actually was a law enforcement officer.

In the end, it came down to Po refusing to divulge the location unless he and Cleo came along. I insisted that where Cleo went, I went. Hank finally did some hand waving and made us special deputies. We borrowed some augment vests and some Steinbauer pneumatic carbines from the TU guys. Deuce had his pulse rifle, and Po selected a couple of stun batons and a wicked looking tactical knife. Within an hour, we were crowded into one of the Tactical Unit personnel carriers, heading for the dropshafts at the end of Armstrong, where it ran into the crater wall. Hank entered the access code for a restricted shaft, and we followed the TU in. Ten decks down, we were on the ragged edge of Freetown, an area of mostly abandoned recycling yards and automated drilling rigs. There was still Tritium under Tycho, but the drills had to go deeper every year.

We rounded up a few squatters and left a man behind to guard them so they couldn't spread the word that the heat was on the way. Po directed us south to where a warren of narrow passages radiated away from the Grissom Street dropshafts. The area had once been relatively prosperous, home to ice miners and tunnel riggers, when these lower decks had supplied most of the water for Tycho City. But the ice deposits had been mined out and the work had gone north to Gagarin Center or Tranquility.

At a junction between two wide feeder tunnels and a branching cluster of residential warrens, Po called a halt. Hank pulled up a map on a small holo display. The warren had several parallel tunnels that converged on the far side, away from us at another feeder junction. Po pointed to a large central compartment, probably a former store or community center. The map showed one way in from our side and two passages out on the far side leading to the junction.

Hank conferred with his TU leader who didn't like the restricted access and noted that there was no direct route to the opposite junction. They also discovered that the surveillance feed from the whole area was offline. They had no eyes on the warren.

I called Rabbit, who was back at the Apollo, on our private link and explained the situation. "Can you tell if the feed has been destroyed or just sliced?"

"No problem, Zack," he said. A second later he replied, "A little of both. The wide area feed was sliced. You should have clear images now." I glanced at Hank who nodded.

"The pickups near the old community center have been physically tampered with or destroyed. There's still an infrared feed from the emergency response beacons in the residential passages, but they can't read through the center bulkhead."

"Thanks, Rabbit. That helps a bit." I signed off but left the link open.

I looked over Hank's shoulder at the visual and infrared images. Nothing moved on the visual, but the infrared picked up heat signatures at the edges of the beacon's range. The emergency beacons were designed to find people holed up in the residences in the event of cave-ins or environmental breaches. They focused on the living quarters, not the community areas. Still, the pickups showed a little of the tunnels as they converged on the common area.

At each of the tunnels the images showed a faint heat signature indicating a sentry. The pattern suggested mutually supporting fields of fire and clear sight line to the only direct entrance from our current position.

The Tactical Unit lead swore softly. "Fast and hard," he said to Boucher. "Not much chance of stealth in there."

Hank signaled to the rest of the unit, and they formed up in two parallel breaching files. Wells attached himself to the right-hand team, tapping the man in front on the shoulder to let him know he was in position.

"Wait," said Po. He drew the stun batons and silently moved off down one of the side tunnels. Hank cursed and moved to stop him, but Cleo held up a hand.

"Let him go, Hank," she whispered. "He knows what he's doing."

We followed him on visual, then on infrared as he quickly penetrated the warren. His heat signature approached the first sentry. They merged for half a second, then withdrew a ways into the narrow tunnel.

Po reappeared and began working his way around to the next tunnel. The sentry remained motionless.

The process repeated itself twice before Po stepped into the visual feed and moved his hand twice in the chopping 'continue mission' signal.

Hank repeated the gesture, and both breaching teams rushed down the corridor. Cleo, Deuce, and I brought up the rear.

It was over almost before the three of us reached the community center. By the time we came through the hatchway, the right-hand team had taken out the remaining sentries and the left-hand team had breached the main room. There was a brief exchange of pneumatic fire, and then the half dozen old men in the room held up their hands in surrender. The unit had them flex cuffed and on their knees in seconds.

The three of us stood around outside the community center with nothing much to contribute, Besides, it spared Hank from having to explain our presence other than as observers.

Hank came over a few minutes later, grinning, and slapped me on the shoulder. "Good intel, Zack. All of these guys have detain-on-sight warrants, and there's enough weaponry here to start a small war. And they had this." He handed me a small round datastick.

"Thanks Hank. I'm glad it went well," I said. Something didn't seem right, though. "But don't you think this was too easy?"

"Well, if that freakish giant of Cleo's hadn't taken out a few of the sentries, it might have gone a lot differently. I'll take the win; easy is just icing on the cake." Hank turned away and began the official recording of the prisoners' faces and biometrics.

Wells and Deuce went off to help organize the weapons and intel seized in the raid, leaving Cleo and me with little to do but watch. Po joined us, his approach so silent that he seemed to just materialize at Cleo's side.

He touched Cleo's shoulder and said something softly to her. She answered in that language that wasn't quite Chinese and they embraced. Then he was gone, exiting as silently as he'd come. Cleo wiped tears from her eyes. I took her hand.

"Everything all right?" I asked.

She tilted her head as if uncertain. "I think so. Po said I'd see him again but not to look for him. It seems he has a few outstanding warrants of his own."

I pulled her close and she held me tightly for a moment.

"I'm not sure I want to see him again," she said, not looking at me. "I love him for being my protector, but I can't forgive him for what he did, turning me into a killing machine."

"But you aren't that anymore." I kissed the top of her head. "If anything, you're the voice of reason and restraint in our little family." She didn't say anything but gave my waist a squeeze.

"Something about this bothers me," I said after a few seconds.

"You mean, why did the Colonel need us?" she asked.

"Yeah." I watched Hank and the team processing the prisoners. "Sure, it was more than the three of us could handle, even with Wells, but it shouldn't have given a squad of seasoned operators much trouble. The Colonel should have been able to mount that kind of operation himself."

"You said he told you his forces were busy elsewhere, maybe out in the Belt," she pointed out.

"Maybe, by all accounts his control out there is pretty solid. All it needed was a single squad, six or seven seasoned operators." I thought for a second. "But if that's all he has with him, he'd be hard pressed to maintain his own security."

Before Cleo could respond, Hank waved at me and motioned me over to where his team was processing the prisoners. "You might want to take a look at this, Zack."

A technician had a data reader up and was scanning through captured data sticks.

"Show him what you just showed me," Hank directed. The technician's hands waved in the air over an interface visible only to him. A series of still images popped up, images from the security feed at the Dai Ichi. I saw Deuce and me approaching the Colonel's table. His personal security scrambler obscured his face, but a red hashmark had been superimposed over his head.

"Show me what else you have," I said.

The images scrolled by, our meeting, Deuce and me leaving, the Colonel waving over his bodyguard, rising and crossing the lobby to the drop shafts. In each image, the colonel was marked with that red hashmark. The bodyguard, the second operator, and a third man who joined them at the dropshaft were each assigned a symbol, possibly a number, in some sort of script that looked like Hanzi but wasn't.

The images ended there, but the implication was clear. The Pathists knew who Metternich was, where he was, and were targeting him. *We weren't eliminating Metternich's competition and recovering data. We were eliminating a threat he didn't have the juice to take care of himself.*

"Thanks," I said to the technician. I moved away, motioning for Hank to follow me. "I'm going to call Zameda and have Rabbit include him in this. Are you good with that?"

"Sure. We're going to wrap up here soon. You just want to rub his nose in it? Want me to help?" Hank's grin was wicked.

"First, I want him to release our assets," I said. "But second, I want him preoccupied for a while. We know where Deuce's daughter is being held, and thanks to your tech, we now know the strength of the opposition."

"Need some back-up?"

I squeezed his arm. "No, we have to do this ourselves. I would appreciate it if you'd run interference with the street patrol if we draw too much attention. I'll get in touch when we have news. Now I need to talk to Rabbit."

Rabbit, true to form, had already been monitoring the raid and knew what I wanted as soon as I opened the link. "Time to stick it to Zameda, Zack?"

"You know it. Open a direct link to his feed." A second later, Zameda's face appeared in my link. "What the hell is going on, Mbele. I'll have you in a Federal lockup before the day is out for this. And who are these people?"

"Gabriel Zameda, meet Lieutenant Henri Boucher, Lunar Security. The jokers in flexcuffs are the Fourfold Path leaders who orchestrated the attack on the Planitia Club. All wrapped up for delivery." My breezy tone hardened. "You can now thank us and release our money. That was the deal, and we've kept our side of it."

"That wasn't the deal," snarled Zameda. "You were supposed to find them and inform me so the FBS could take them."

"No, we were to find them and make sure they were taken down. I can have Rabbit play back our exact conversation if you like." I smiled. "Relax, Gabe. I'm sure Lieutenant Boucher will be happy to keep the FBS in the picture, and even give credit where it's due. You did discover the Path was here on the Moon, after all."

"Of course," Hank chimed in. "The charges against these guys are Federal, anyway. We're always happy to assist the FBS."

Zameda's face puckered as if he'd tasted something

rotten. "Where will you be taking them?"

"South Freetown Station. It's the closest one with a big enough holding facility. Downloading directions to you now."

"I'll meet you there with a team and warrant authorizing the FBS to assume custody," said Zameda.

"That's the spirit," I said. "And Gabe, don't forget the money." I broke the link before he could respond.

"Sorry to leave you with that prick, Hank, but we've got to get moving."

He waved me off. "No problem. I'll get credit for the bust and he'll get the headache of filing the charges. Give 'em hell, Zack. Let me know when Deuce's daughter is safe."

I picked up Cleo and Deuce and we waved Wells over.

"What was that about?" Cleo asked.

"The Colonel is isolated," I said once Wells had joined us. "The Pathists had images from the security feed at the Dai Ichi marking the Colonel and his bodyguards. The two we saw, a third and likely a fourth or fifth covering the suite where Ingrid and Grace are. They were planning an attack on him. We were his preemptive strike." I paused as they processed that. "Those four or five operators are all the forces he has. The rest of the Revenants have deserted him or gone freelance."

"Zack, are you sure?" Cleo shook her head. "We saw more than that on Highpoint."

"Did we?" I counted on my fingers. "Two at the bar where they met Deuce, the one in the storefront that I killed, two to carry Ingrid and keep her sedated and two more to cover their escape. No more."

"Let's get these *bautu*," rumbled Deuce.

"We've got to move fast. We have to assume the Colonel will have some way of knowing the Path has been neutralized. We need to get to him before they can move

Grace and Ingrid."

"Why would they move them," asked Wells.

"To maintain control of the exchange," Cleo answered before I could. "It's what I'd do." She looked at me and nodded. "Right, let's go."

"Nonlethal ammo only," I said as we trotted off toward the dropshafts. "We can't risk hurting Grace or Ingrid."

We made our way back up to Armstrong and Rabbit directed an ordinary taxi to our location. If the cheap AI pilot thought anything of four heavily armed patrons directing it to the Promenade lifts, it stayed quiet. I'm also sure Rabbit jammed its coms and wiped its recent memory as we got out.

We reached the service shafts and Wells flashed his FBS credentials to get us on.

"Where's Grace, Rabbit?" I asked over our link.

"I pinged her implant less than a minute ago," he said. "Level 36 above the Dai Ichi lobby. One of two suites, 3604 or 3606. The trace is only accurate to about a ten-meter radius."

The service shaft took us to the lobby level behind the concierge area. Rabbit tapped the security system and fed the images to our links.

"Anyone see anything?" Cleo whispered. "I've got nothing."

"Nothing here," said Wells as he scanned his quarter of the lobby.

"Odd," I said. "Rabbit, anyone light up on your scan?"

"No, Zack," he said. "Just a bunch of civilians milling about."

I considered pulling back and taking the service lifts up but decided against it. If the Colonel had no security in the lobby, he was hunkered down in the suite, and the quicker we got up there the better. Still, someone needed eyes on that route.

"Wells, take the service lift in case they try to slip out that way. Deuce and Cleo, on me. We'll take the main lifts to the 35th level, then the stairs up from opposite ends of the passageway." Cleo nodded agreement and Deuce grunted. Wells was already moving toward the service areas. He kept in touch over the link but encountered no opposition up to the 35th level.

We drew some stares but no direct confrontation as we crossed the lobby. I'm sure the front desk staff called both their private and Lunar Security, but I counted on Hank to run interference for us.

We piled out on the 35th level and I sent Cleo down the passageway to link up with Wells. Once we were in position, we climbed the emergency stairwell to the 36th.

We stacked at the doors to the passageway leading to the suites and I called Rabbit. "Have you got eyes on the 36th level?"

"Negative," he said. "It's not jammed or sliced. The feeds have been physically disabled. Sorry Zack, even the infrared is down."

"No surprise," I muttered. "Okay, team. Hard and fast, on three. One, two, three!"

We burst through the doors, sighting over our weapons and rushed down the passageway toward the suites Rabbit had marked on our heads-ups. The empty passageway. No Black Ops commandos, no security, no housekeeping staff with concealed pneumatics. No one.

We reached the door to suite 3606 and found it ajar. The others stacked behind me. I sighted over my Steinbauer and nudged the door open with my toe.

"Come in, Zachariah," said Colonel Metternich. "We have a lot to talk about."

Chapter 23

I pushed the door open, but it stopped halfway when it struck the body on the floor. I glanced down and recognized one of the men who'd been with the Colonel at our meeting in the lobby. He stared up at me through sightless eyes that seemed fixed on the small hole in the middle of his forehead.

I paused and swept the room left and right but saw nothing else. Metternich sat in a wing backed chair facing the door. He held a silver Huang pneumatic pistol pointed toward but not quite at Grace and Ingrid who sat on a short sofa opposite him.

I lifted my carbine to cover him as Deuce fanned out to my left, pulse rifle at the ready. "Put the weapon down, Colonel."

He looked down at the Huang. "Yes, I suppose I should." He leaned forward slowly and placed the pistol on the carpeted floor at his feet.

I rushed forward and nudged it well out of reach. Deuce lifted his rifle and held out a hand to Grace. She lifted Ingrid in her arms and ran to his side. He enfolded them in an embrace and moved them to the far side of the room whispering softly to them. Meanwhile, Cleo and Wells checked the rest of the suite and nodded all clear.

Metternich sat calmly in the chair, his hands with the palms up in his lap. I lowered the Steinbauer. "What happened here, Colonel?"

"Shortly after our meeting, I decided to release my remaining security staff from my service. I thanked each of them and paid them a generous separation bonus, enough to set themselves up in any new endeavor they might choose." He smiled at me. "You see, Zachariah, I was that confident that you'd neutralize the Fourfold Path and ensure my short-term safety."

"As to that, we had help," I said.

"But the job got done. Xander, Isaac, Bradley and Midori all took the payoff and went out on their own. I doubt they will be any further trouble to the authorities."

I gestured to the body by the door. "What about him?"

Metternich sighed. "Damien couldn't accept the new reality. He wanted to continue the fight. I was forced to take more radical measures." He shook his head. "I truly regret that. Damien was a true believer, fervent in his dedication to the Martian Way."

"And what is the 'new reality,' Colonel?" I asked softly. I had been a true believer myself before the Bear and Metternich's biotanks burned it out of me.

"The Way is dead, Zachariah," he answered sadly. "The lure of easy money and power proved stronger than dedication to any cause. Most of the First Battalion is either dead or splintered into rival gangs fighting for control of the Belt. The FBS has seized our embryos, even though they have no idea what they have. And Ulan Bator has reneged on our financial backing, leaving me without resources. The datastick you have is only valuable if one has the resources to develop new clones."

"What do you want from us? Sympathy? A fresh start?" I jammed the muzzle of the Steinbauer into his chest. "I swore an oath to kill you, an oath I've renewed almost every day since the Bear."

Metternich lifted his hands and looked up at me. "I'm at your mercy."

My hands gripped the carbine so tightly they shook. I could feel my finger tighten on the trigger. *Do it!* a voice screamed in my head, the same voice that had screamed and cried for rescue from the burning pain of the biotank.

"Zack, don't," whispered Cleo. "Don't do it."

I retightened my grip on the trigger and pushed the muzzle harder into his chest, forcing him back deeper into the chair. Then I let out a long-held breath and stepped back, lowering the carbine. "You left me. You left me in that place, turned me into a freak, used me again to serve your twisted vision, and now you want me to ensure your safety? When will it be enough, Colonel?"

"It ends here, Zachariah." His voice was gentle, almost fatherly. "I surrender myself to you and your team. Do what you will. Kill me, take out all your anger on me, or perhaps turn me over to higher authorities. My best hope for survival lies with the FBS."

"The FBS?" I couldn't believe Metternich would turn himself over to the Feds. Then it hit me. "You bastard. You set this whole thing up. You tipped Zameda about the kidnapping, made it look like the Path was trying to get to Cleo. You needed us to do what you didn't have the juice to handle. You played us all."

"You give me too much credit," he said with a shrug. "I gave Zameda some information, and he drew his own conclusions."

"I should turn you over to him. You two deserve each other." I pulled flexcuffs from my belt. "Hands behind your back, Colonel."

He complied, smiling the whole time like an indulgent parent. "You always were the best of us, Zachariah."

I cinched the cuffs. "And look what that got me. Playacting for rich charters who want to believe there's romance in life on the edge rather than desperation and poverty. Either that or dealing with the likes of Colin Jones and Kwai Hong so I can stay one step ahead of the banks and the law. What a life."

Cleo stepped up and touched my arm. "It's the life we chose, isn't it?"

I sighed and squeezed her hand and answered. "The life we chose."

"LT," Deuce called. "If it's all the same to you, I'm gonna get Grace and Ingrid out of here. We'll hook up back at the Apollo."

I considered whether I needed him here but a glance at the strain on Grace's face convinced me that Deuce was right. "Go, get them situated. I'll deal with this. Cleo, you go with them." She looked like she was going to object but saw the same need in Grace and just nodded.

"What about me, Zack?" asked Wells.

"I'm about to call your old boss to come take custody of the Colonel here." I grinned. "You want to be in on that?"

"Wouldn't miss it."

I opened a link to Rabbit. "Rabbit, we're good here. Deuce and Cleo are taking Grace and Ingrid back to the Apollo. I have the Colonel in cuffs. I need to get Zameda up here."

"Why is he still alive, Zack?" Rabbit's voice was a low growl. "We agreed he needed to die."

I stared down at Metternich trying to muster the hatred that had driven my life since the Bear but all I felt was an overwhelming sadness. "It's complicated, Rabbit.

Just get Zameda on the feed."

Zameda appeared in my link a second later, looking harried. "What the hell, Mbele? What do you want. I've issued the release order; you'll have your funds shortly."

"Now, Gabe, I'm trying to do you a good turn here. You have staff people who can handle booking the Pathists. I'm offering you an honest to God war criminal." I said. "Dai Ichi Hotel, on the Promenade, Suite 3606."

"What war criminal?" he demanded. "Why should I believe you?"

"A name you'll know, guaranteed. Come on, Gabe, this is your ticket to that staff job Earthside." I paused, letting him stew for a moment. "Dai Ichi, 3606. Wells and I will be waiting."

To Zameda's credit, he made good time. No sooner had Deuce and Cleo pinged us that they were safe at the Apollo, than Zameda was pounding on the suite door. I opened it and he pushed his way in followed by two FBS operators in full battle rattle. They swept the room but pulled up when they spied Wells leaning against the opposite wall.

"Hey, Tad," said Wells to the man on the left.

"Hey, Goon," the man answered, lowering his weapon and signaling his counterpart to do the same.

"Mbele," Zameda surveyed the room, focusing on Metternich sitting in the armchair with his hands behind his back. "Is this the dangerous war criminal you promised?"

I stood close to the Colonel, establishing which of us was in control. "Special Agent Gabriel Zameda meet Colonel Hans Metternich, former Director of Martian Special Forces and prior President for Life of the Martian Republic."

Zameda looked blankly at me for a moment before laughing out loud. "What kind of joke is this, Mbele? Who is this joker, and what do you hope to get out of this."

Metternich spoke up, his voice soft, almost friendly. "I assure you, Agent Zameda, that Zachariah is being completely truthful. I am indeed Hans Wilhelm Metternich. I assume you or one of your men has a portable retinal scanner or DNA probe. I invite you to use them to verify my identity."

Zameda looked nonplussed, then angry. He waved to the operator Wells had called Tad. The man stepped forward and withdrew a small instrument from his utility vest. He positioned it in front of Metternich's right eye and activated it. It beeped softly and he lifted it to look at its read-out.

His bored expression vanished. "Holy shit," he said. He repeated the process. Again, the device beeped, and he checked it, his face growing pale.

"Uh, sir?" he stammered. "According to this, his story is *honto.* This guy really is Metternich."

"Impossible." Zameda snatched the reader away from his agent and repeated the retinal scan a third time. He stared at the read-out and breathed out very slowly. He looked from the Colonel to me and back again. "How is this possible?"

"Reports of the Colonel's death were premature. I even thought I'd killed him myself," I said. "He escaped Mars and for the past several years has been operating with what was left of the First Battalion out in the Belt. Now, his forces have dwindled through attrition and the lure of easy money, and he's had a change of heart. He wants to surrender to the Federal Bureau of Security." I paused and smiled. "That's you, Gabriel."

"Why now? Why not take a share of this easy money and lay low, live in comfort, rather than in a cell in Antarctica?"

"Because aside from the Fourfold Path, I have

many enemies," replied Metternich pleasantly. "Various factions from my former subordinates, not to mention the remnants of several criminal gangs with whom I have had dealings. All would be happy to kill me on sight. No, I think my best chance of survival is in custody, even if that's in a cell."

After a long minute, Zameda drew himself up. "Hans Metternich, I'm placing you under lawful detention for war crimes. You are cautioned that any statements you make may be taken down and used in evidence against you." He droned through the rest of the mandatory cautions and statement of rights. I tuned it out; it was all formality anyway. Lawyers would be stepping all over each other to be the superstar who represented the infamous Colonel Metternich.

Zameda concluded his spiel, and the Colonel nodded his understanding. Tad and his partner stepped up and assisted him to his feet. They started for the door and Zameda seemed to notice Wells for the first time. "Fall in, Wells. We'll discuss your future with the FBS back at HQ."

"No, I don't think so." Wells settled the Steinbauer on his hip. "You'll have my resignation in the morning." He looked at me and I nodded. We'd make a place for him.

Zameda hardly paused, sneered. "So be it."

Metternich smirked as he watched. "I'll be seeing you, Zachariah."

"On the tenth of never, Colonel. On the tenth of never." I said, returning his smile.

Chapter 24

The door slammed behind Zameda and company, and I turned to Wells. “Goon?”

He grinned and shrugged. “My real name’s Gideon. Never liked it much. I had just reported to my first command, and they were mounting an operation against some supply types selling military hardware on the black market. Top Sergeant was assigning teams and didn’t know me, so he told one of the guys to ‘take the goon and make sure he stays out of the way.’ Name stuck, and it’s been Goon ever since.”

“Well, Goon,” I said. “Welcome aboard. Let’s join the rest of the crew.”

We made our way back to the Apollo. I asked Rabbit to call the Port Authority and have the *Profit* moved to our regular berth. There was no further need for stealth, and it had likely been all for nothing anyway. On the way I used the public access link to call Sam Guthrie.

“Mbele,” he said answering the call. “What news?”

“You’ll hear about it over the newsnet before long, but

the job is done. The Pathists who ordered the hit on the Planitia are in custody. None got away."

"I'd have preferred dead," observed Guthrie.

"I would, too, Sam. But they were well dug in. I had to have help from the local law to pull it off. Boucher's an honest cop. He'll make sure they get what's due."

"It's done then," said Guthrie. "Thank you. Don't take this wrong, but I don't think I want to see you again."

"I understand," I answered. "We only used about half of the fifty thousand you advanced us. How should I get the balance to you?"

"Keep it," said Guthrie. "God knows you earned it. Good-bye, Zack."

"Good-bye, Sam."

By the time we reached the Apollo, Rabbit had arranged for the *Profit* to be moved. We'd be back in our usual berth in a few hours. I found Cleo and Rabbit in the sitting area drinking coffee. Deuce, Grace and Ingrid had retired to one of the bedrooms with the door closed. Wells and I stripped off our gear and took turns in the shower. Clean and dressed in fresh clothes we joined Cleo and Rabbit.

"Metternich is in custody. Zameda took the deal, and our funds should be released by now," I said to Cleo.

Wells read Cleo's expression and retired to the empty bedroom 'to give us some space.'

"Deuce will want to talk with you," Cleo said softly as she handed me a cup of coffee. I sipped and found it generously laced with good Martian whiskey. I squeezed her hand. "I know. Thank you."

"We need to talk as well." She must have seen the alarmed look on my face because she kissed me lightly and said, "Relax, nothing bad."

"You should know, I've asked Wells to join the team. His friends call him Goon."

She thought for a second. "He should be a good fit.

We'll make him a formal offer once we get back to the ship."

Deuce opened the door to their bedroom. Inside, Ingrid lay asleep on the bed with Grace sitting beside her. Deuce closed the door and faced me.

"LT? Need a word."

"Sure, Deuce," I said. "Here or in the other room?"

He crossed to the other bedroom, and I followed.

"Give us the room, Goon?" I said.

Wells nodded to Deuce and left the room to us, closing the door behind him. Once in the room, Deuce seemed to shrink somehow. He faced me but looked at his feet, not meeting my eye.

"How long we been together, LT? Ten years?" he asked.

"About that, since Basic."

"You got me through Basic, LT," he said softly. "I swore then I'd never let you down. Even when you were in the Bear, I kept a watch as best I could. Came to get you as soon as the war ended."

"I know, Deuce. I wouldn't have made it without knowing you were out there, waiting. You don't owe me anything. I owe you." He continued to stare at his feet, shuffling a little. "Say what you need to say, Deuce. I already know or guessed most of it."

"Thing is, LT, Grace and me, we have a kid now. She needs a home, a safe place. I can't be travelin' all over the system, maybe gettin' in the way of Kwai Hong, or the rest of the First. I never thought I'd want a family, but now I got one, and I don't wanna give it up. Grace and me talked it out. We'll get married as soon as we can and find a place here on the Moon. Mariko's got contacts. She'll help us get jobs. Grace can always find gigs in the clubs up above. We'll get by."

"I've only got one thing to say, Deuce," I said with a grin. "We'd better get an invite to the wedding."

Then he did meet my eye, with tears in his. "You know it, Zack." He stepped forward and embraced me, threatening to crush the wind out of me, but in a good way.

"There's one other thing," I said when I could breathe again. "Talk to Cleo. You're not exactly poor, you know. You and Grace will do more than 'get by.'"

It took Cleo nearly an hour to convince Deuce he was entitled to a quarter of our newly released assets, both the stocks and the cash reserves. He and Grace worked with Cleo to come up with a system of scheduled payments and equity holdings that avoided the worst of the tax hits. She convinced him to hold his quarter share of the ship as an investment and possible income source, should they need it. The totals were enough for a nice place in Upper Armstrong with plenty of room for a growing family. Grace and Cleo hugged and promised to stay in touch. Rabbit booked them a suite at a nice long-term stay warren just north of the port, and the three of them left to buy some new clothes for Grace and Ingrid. Deuce said he'd be by in a day or so to clear out his workshop.

The room seemed empty as the door closed behind them. Or maybe it was that part of my heart where Deuce had lived for the past ten years. Cleo wrapped her arms around me from behind and held me close. That helped.

Rabbit stayed quiet in the corner, but I noticed he'd turned his chair away from us and his virtual interface was closed.

"Everything Jake, Rabbit?" I asked.

"I knew he'd leave." Rabbit's voice almost broke, but he took a deep breath. "As soon as I saw her, I knew. Deuce doesn't like people most of the time. He barely tolerates me, but she was different. I could see it, the way he looked at her. It's like the way you look at Cleo. But she's not like Cleo. Ship life isn't for that one. And now they have a kid. I knew he'd leave."

"Deuce will stay in touch," Cleo said. "You know he will."

"I know. But it won't be the same."

She walked over and put a hand on his shoulder. "I know. But Zack and I won't be leaving you. You're stuck with us."

The Port Authority sent us a message a short time later that the *Profit* had been positioned in our usual berth and needed only our activation code to hook up to shore services. Rabbit sent it and we gathered up our clothes and gear to head home.

Goon joined us and made a point of talking quietly with Rabbit for a few minutes. Whatever he said seemed to make Rabbit happy because soon they were laughing at some joke or other.

Sylvia welcomed us home with a cold shoulder. She resented being tied to the ship while we 'got to have all the fun.' I sighed. It was good to be home.

We sat down with Goon and made him a formal offer to join the crew. He was surprised to learn the terms included a quarter share in any new cash income and new stock purchases as well as an option to buy an equity position in the rest of our holdings.

"That's a lot more generous than I expected," he said.

"Not generous," Cleo replied. "Practical. You're invested this way, not just a hired gun. We'll need to work out berthing for you unless you want to bunk with Rabbit."

"Oh, I'm happy in Deuce's space once he gets his gear cleared out. I can use the workshop for gunsmithing and weapons maintenance. I'm not the engineer he is, but I know my way around a toolbox."

"Sounds good," I said. "Didn't know you were an armorer."

"Level 3 certified," Goon said proudly.

"We don't have shipboard weapons, but the personal arms can use your services."

That pretty much settled it with Goon. We unpacked and stowed gear and clothes, and Rabbit got busy in the galley, making us a meal. None of us had eaten much in the past day or so.

I went forward to the cockpit and sat in the command seat. At first Sylvia ignored me, but after a few minutes she couldn't keep from saying something.

"Deuce is really leaving us?" she asked.

"Yes. I think he'd been looking for something for a while. This respectable life was chafing on him. Grace will be the anchor he needs to keep his focus."

"What about you, Zack? Are you happy being respectable?"

I didn't answer her. The truth was, respectability wore thin when you had to live it every day.

Cleo put our name on the open charter list and started trolling the commercial net for business. We were well stocked with provisions, and a check of the induction coils showed them to be in good shape, well over ninety percent capacity despite our abusing them on the recent run from Highpoint.

Goon settled in nicely after Deuce cleared his personal gear out of the workshop. We all gathered in the salon for a farewell meal. Tears were shed and promises made, but truth be told, I'd never seen Deuce so relaxed and happy.

About ten days after Zameda took Metternich away, I sat in the cockpit command chair looking out over the spaceport in the late lunar day. Cleo hadn't had any luck finding us a charter, but I don't think she was trying very hard. We went out to eat almost every night, just the two of us, exploring the restaurants and clubs along Armstrong like young kids, experiencing the courtship we never had.

"We're being hailed, Zack," Sylvia said as I was about

to drift off to sleep. "An FBS Director named Jackson wants to speak to you."

"Put him on, Sylvia." I rubbed my eyes and focused.

The cockpit screen lit up, and a tall man in a well-cut business suit stood below the nose of the ship. "This is Zack Mbele," I said. "You wanted to speak to me?"

"Captain Mbele," he said holding up a credentials case with his ID. "I'm FBS Director Silas Jackson. I'd like to speak to you and Ms. Lee. Do I have your permission to come aboard?"

I was impressed that he asked and intrigued by what he might have to say. "Permission granted, starboard sally port." I swung out of the chair and crossed the catwalk to the ladder. The sally port opened, and Jackson entered. He stepped into the hold, hands at his sides, palms open, moving slowly but smoothly.

"Welcome aboard, Mr. Jackson," I said. "Come up to the salon."

I watched as he climbed the ladder. He moved well, smooth and steady, no hesitation, but no hurry either. This was a man who was used to both action and command. I decided to give him a fair hearing. We sat in the salon and Cleo joined us.

"What can we do for you, Director Jackson? By the way, how's Gabriel Zameda doing?"

He laughed. "Gabriel is on his way Earthside to a staff job where he can't get into too much trouble. With his family connection, he'll probably end up in the Senate or Secretary of something or other in a few years."

"Why are you here, Mr. Jackson," Cleo asked.

"Hans Metternich sends his regards," he said. "He also has made us an intriguing offer."

"Why do you need me, then," I said. "I don't care if Colonel Metternich spends the rest of his life in a cell in Antarctica or gets tossed out the nearest airlock."

Jackson smiled at that. "I wouldn't mourn him either. However, between pre-War Martian Intelligence and his post-War activities, he's gathered a wealth of information about some very bad people. He knows where to find some serious war criminals, knows who runs most of the drug and weapons smuggling in and out of Mars, and has a long list of other information that we'd love to get our hands on. He's offered to share it with us in return for some concessions to his comfort and upkeep."

"How does this concern me? Sounds like he's pulling a scam to save his own skin." I crossed my arms, a defensive posture, but I didn't want to buy what Jackson was selling.

"He's given us a few samples that panned out in the apprehension of some serious players. Enough to prove he's got the goods." Jackson said. "But he won't give up any more to us. He says he'll only talk to you."

"No, absolutely not." I shook my head. *No, not again Colonel. I won't be part of your scheming anymore.* "I won't be your go between. I don't want to talk to that man again."

Jackson held up his hands. "Just hear me out. We don't want you to be our interrogator, or just a go between. We want to hire you and your crew to go after some of these people."

"We're not bounty hunters," said Cleo.

"Again, hear me out," said Jackson. "We propose to set you up as a special agency within the FBS, outside the chain of command, under my personal direction. Zack would get the specifics on a target from Metternich, and you'd have final say as to who and what you would go after. You'll have the full support of FBS resources, but you'll also have complete freedom of action. Just get the job done."

I started to tell him to stick it, but Cleo held up a

hand. "What does it pay?"

"You'll be authorized by the Federal government to seize any money or property obtained illegally by your target. Money will go directly to fund your activity; property will be sold in Federal auctions and the proceeds deposited in your accounts." He reached into his jacket and pulled out a small data screen. "The agreement and asset forfeiture documents are on this screen." He held it out. "Look it over."

Cleo took it and read through it quickly. "I'll need a copy of this, and Zack and I will need some time to discuss it with our other partners."

"Of course." Jackson grinned. "Download it to your link and read it carefully. Talk to Conejo and Wells." Then he grew serious. "But I'll need an answer within twelve hours. After that, I'll have to transfer Metternich to Corrections, and he'll be on his way to Antarctica."

He stood and extended his hand. "I'll give you a chance to discuss it. My direct link is in the document. I'll find my own way out if Sylvia will open the lock for me."

"Sylvia," I called.

"Done, Zack," she said. A minute later she said, "He's gone. Are you going to take his offer? The terms are wide open. We could make a load of money from this, a lot more than the charter business."

"Give me a break, Sylvia," I pleaded. "I haven't seen the offer yet."

"But she's right, Zack," said Cleo. "The possibilities are wide open. So is the risk."

"So what do you want to do?" I asked her.

"That's not fair, Zack. This isn't up to me alone."

"No," I said. "But what you want is all that matters to me. Look, Cleo, I know that all you ever wanted was a stable home and business, something that had some permanence. I get that. And if that's what it takes for me to be with you, I'll do it. I'll smile and make small talk and grow out the dreadlocks and play the dashing charter boat captain."

Her face softened and she touched my cheek. "But you'll hate every minute of it. After this episode with Ingrid and Grace, I can see that. You need the action. You thrive on it. Truth be told, even I found the settled life a bit boring. Uncle Po reminded me what I was trained to do. I can't be what I was, but maybe together we can do some good."

I took her in my arms, and we held each other. "Do you think we can find a way to do both?" I asked. She laughed. "What?" I said, pulling away to look at her.

"It seems Jackson anticipated that. He encourages us to maintain the charter business as a cover, and legitimate business between missions. So, yes, we'll do both."

We called Goon and Rabbit to the salon and Cleo laid out the offer from Jackson.

Goon shrugged, "I'm the new guy, but for what it's worth, if this is legit, we should do it."

Rabbit nodded. "I'm in. Whatever you guys decide as long as we stay together. Will I still get to do the cooking?"

Cleo and I laughed. "Unless Goon's talents include gourmet chef," I said.

"The job's all yours," Goon said to Rabbit. "Just leave the guns to me."

We sat quietly for a few minutes. "So, what's it going to be like working for the FBS?" I asked Goon. "Any pointers?"

"Technically, we're not FBS employees," said Cleo. "We're a self-funded agency within the Special Activities department directly under Jackson. This document and the forfeiture authority it gives us makes us privateers."

Goon, Rabbit, and I exchanged looks and said in unison, "Space Pirates!"

OPERATING PROFIT

A story from the ongoing *Profit* logbooks

The spaceport at Gagarin Center had been built long before the Unification War when the Center was a modest Lunar settlement mainly involved in biochip manufacturing. The War and the postwar economic boom increased the demand for the chips, and chip manufacturing boomed along with it. Gagarin Center almost doubled in size in five years. Unfortunately, living space, infrastructure, and the Port hadn't. Several big construction projects were underway, including a domed spaceport, but for now, the old surface port did its best to keep up with the traffic.

I supposed we were lucky the *Profit* was small enough to fit into the VIP traffic section of the Port. If we'd been berthed on the Commercial side, we'd have had a two-kilometer drive from ship to terminal. As it was, we were a little more than 200 meters from the terminal airlock. I'd gotten soft as a charter boat captain, accustomed to berthing in VIP ports as befitted our rich clientele.

Profit had started her life as a fast interceptor for the

Martian Navy. I'd stolen her in the chaos that followed the collapse of the Martian Republic and paid premium *yuan* to have registration and ownership papers forged for her. I'd struggled for a few years to make a living running cargo and doing some occasional smuggling until we'd taken money from a big score and upgraded *Profit's* cabins and salon into a high-class charter boat. We played off our reputation as reformed smugglers and pirates to attract clients who liked the illusion of danger in their charters.

"What are we doing here, Zack?" asked Sylvia, the ship's AI.

"Orders from the FBS, Sylvia," I said through my link implant as I slid down the ladder to the main deck. "This is apparently where they're holding the Colonel. It looks like it's time for us to start earning our keep."

We'd dropped off our last charter at Tycho City two standard days ago. Cleo, my ex-wife and current business partner had put us on the available charter list, and we'd taken a bit of shore leave in our home port. That's when Special Agent Jackson had called with our first assignment. A couple of months earlier, I'd taken a Devil's bargain with the Federal Bureau of Security. I'd turned over Colonel Metternich and agreed to work as a privateer for the Bureau tracking down war criminals and gangsters the Colonel knew about and could finger for us.

Cleo and Gideon Wells, Goon to his friends and our newest crewmate, were already on the deck, waiting for me. Even though this wasn't an operational mission, Cleo had dressed in a black jump suit, her stun batons strapped to her back. Goon had chosen dark pants and shirt with a shoulder holster and a Czeck and Hawley needler with pneumatic boost.

"This is a meet and greet," I said. "Not a war."

"You never know, Zack," said Goon. "The last time we met the Colonel, things got pretty tense."

I crossed the deck and thumbed the lock on the weapons locker. I drew a Steinbauer pneumatic and strapped a pair of throwing knives to my wrists. Cleo gave me a wry smile as I closed the locker. I shrugged. "You never know."

We climbed into our ground car and sealed the canopy. "Ready to depressurize, Sylvia," I said. "Rabbit, track us please."

"No worries, Zack," said Rabbit from his post in the salon. "Tracking and recording. See you on the downside, Goon."

"Not if I see you first, Rabbit." Goon settled into the rear seat.

Eddie Conejo, Eddie the Rabbit or just Rabbit, was a data slicer who'd once shared a cell with me in Brunault prison. His programming and slicing talents were unrivaled, and his talents as a chef made our charter business one of the most popular between the Earth and the Moon. He and Goon had become unlikely friends in the two months Goon had been aboard.

Sylvia depressurized the cargo bay and lowered the forward ramp. We rolled out and turned right to take the pathway to the Terminal. A couple of minutes later, we joined a short queue of other travelers waiting for the lock to open. Ten minutes after that, we parked in a visitor's space in the Spaceport Customs lot and climbed out.

"We're supposed to meet Jackson here at the Customs Office," said Cleo after a quick review of his summons. She stepped closer to the walkway leading to the Office. "He doesn't say anything about the Colonel."

"It's about the Colonel all right." I set the security lock on the ground car and followed her. "Jackson wouldn't call otherwise, and I've got a bad feeling in my gut like I always get when meeting Metternich."

As if on cue, my link chimed with a request to accept

an encrypted message. I approved it and heard Jackson's voice through the implant. "I see you're all here. Good, it'll save repetition. In a few seconds, a black ground car will pull up next to you. The driver's recognition signal will be October second; you will get into the vehicle and be brought to your destination. And tell Conejo that the vehicle has better masking than even he can slice, so don't waste the effort."

"Is all this necessary, Agent Jackson?" I asked. "I would think we'd earned a little trust here."

"Oh, I trust you, Zack," he said. "I trust Cleo and Goon and even Conejo when it comes to you and the ship. But there are a lot of other people on both sides of the law who would like to see the Colonel in the ground. It's them I don't trust." He cut the connection. Ten seconds later, the promised ground car pulled into the lot and stopped in front of Cleo.

A driver in a dark business suit and dark glasses climbed out and opened the rear passenger door. "October second," was all he said. I shrugged and climbed in the back, sliding over to make room for Cleo and Goon. The windows opaqued as soon as the driver started forward.

"Not sure I like this, Zack." Goon fidgeted with his jacket, adjusting it so he could reach the shoulder holster. "Blind spins in government vehicles rarely end well."

"Don't worry, Goon," I said with confidence I didn't feel. "We're valuable assets. Jackson needs us more than we need him."

"Right," agreed Cleo. All right, so her tone was sarcastic, but she did agree.

The ride was short but convoluted enough that I couldn't tell where we were. If we'd been in Tycho City, I'd have been able to follow the route by time and turns. I wasn't as familiar with Gagarin Center.

Eventually, we slowed and heard the sounds of a gate

or door being opened. We descended at least two levels before rolling to a stop. The windows cycled to clear, and I saw that we were in a garage or warehouse of some sort. Our driver jumped out and held the door for us as we climbed out. Jackson stood near the front of the ground car. He waved a dismissal to the driver who climbed back in and pulled away.

"Hello Zack, Cleo," Jackson said pleasantly. He stepped forward and extended his hand to Goon. "Agent Wells, I see you've thrown in with these pirates. Welcome."

Goon glanced at me before shaking Jackson's hand. "Thanks. Where the hell are we?"

Jackson chuckled as he gestured toward a double door a few meters away. "This was a Federal supply depot during the war. It was abandoned a few years ago and put on the market. The FBS bought it. On the levels above, a legitimate corporation is building office and retail space. Here in the sub-levels, the FBS maintains a detention facility for high priority detainees."

"It's a black site," said Cleo.

"We prefer to think of it as an unobtrusive detention facility," said Jackson without a trace of irony. He pushed open one of the doors and waved us through. We entered a long corridor with concrete floor and overhead and smoothed regolith walls. The passage ended at a pressure bulkhead with a central hatch. Jackson cycled the hatch and led us through into a large space at least forty meters on a side and ten high. Catwalks and guard stations lined the walls about halfway between the floor and the overhead. They all focused on a single clear-walled cell in the center of the compartment.

Colonel Hans Metternich sat in a bare metal chair in the middle of the cell. Behind him a bunk made up tight in military fashion stood against the back wall. Off to one side, a metal sink flanked a toilet, all in plain view of the guards on the catwalk. A second chair faced the cell from the outside. Jackson pointed to me and then to the chair.

The Colonel smiled at me as I sat down. "Hello Zachariah. Don't look so distressed at my reduced circumstances. Agent Jackson assures me that positive results from my little tips will result in improved accommodations."

"What have you got for us, Colonel?" My voice was harsher than I'd intended.

He smiled indulgently. "I know this is difficult for you, Zachariah. But I do believe we'll make a good team."

"What have you got for us, Colonel?" I repeated.

"So, down to business." The Colonel crossed his legs, shifting in the hard chair. "In ten days, Colonel Tobias Schecter will arrive at Tharsis Docks on Mars. He's a wanted war criminal and currently runs most of the sex trade in the inner Belt."

"Colonel Schecter is dead, killed in the assault on Planitia Base," I said.

"Are you certain?" Metternich asked. "Did you see his body? I was officially dead for several years, yet here I am, resurrected."

I looked at Jackson who shrugged. "We've heard rumors but nothing actionable. For what it's worth, Schecter was just assumed to have died in the bombardment of the Base HQ. Several survivors attested to it, but they were never closely interrogated."

I turned back to the Colonel. "So, a war criminal will be at Tharsis Docks in ten days. Why would he come to Mars?"

"He's meeting his Banker," said the Colonel. "Money is great, but when you're a wanted war criminal it's hard to spend it. So, he has to make it clean and invest it in anonymous accounts and real estate. The profits come back to a dummy corporation based on Highpoint. He has a numbered account he draws on under a false identity."

"This 'Banker' takes his own cut, I assume," I said.

"Of course. He's a facilitator who has operated in Tharsis since long before the Revolution," said the Colonel. "I've used his services myself."

"The Banker isn't your target," said Jackson from behind me. "Schecter is."

I turned in the chair. "What's in it for us?"

Jackson crossed his arms and frowned. "Besides fulfilling your contract and taking down a monster who condemned thousands of women and girls to the worst nightmare imaginable?"

He was right, and I knew we'd take the mission, but I had a point to make. "We're supposed to be self-funding through seizure of assets. We need operating capital to keep the *Profit* flying. Sitting here with you or taking out war criminals on Mars doesn't pay the bills."

"There's a reward for Schecter's arrest," said Jackson. "And some compensation for your expenses may be reimbursable. This mission is a proof of concept. I answer to superiors who aren't totally convinced our contract will pay off."

"We'll take the job," I said. "As you say, proof of concept. But this is the last free ride you get. The contract also lets us refuse an assignment without explanation." I turned back to Metternich. "What more can you tell us, Colonel? Schecter's security arrangements? Where he's meeting this 'Banker'? Anything to give us a jump on him. I don't relish a gunfight on the Docks, or worse, in some crowded warren."

"Agent Jackson has all the particulars, Zachariah." Metternich cocked his head. "I will tell you that he travels with at least three security guards as well as personal weapons. He usually meets the Banker at an office in Upper Beta, a location with both high visibility and high security. Your best option to take him is in transit between locations or possibly at his hotel."

"Anything else?"

Metternich smiled wryly. "You'll know what needs to be done when you get to Tharsis. Farewell, Zachariah. We'll talk again soon."

I knew a dismissal when I heard one. I could sit there as long as I liked, but the Colonel wouldn't say anything more. I rose and walked away toward the bulkhead. Cleo and Goon fell in behind me. Jackson hurried to catch up. He handed me a datastick.

"That's all the information we have on Schecter: security, aliases, what schedule we could piece together. The mission is capture and return. We want this guy alive."

I took the datastick. "Take us back to the Customs Office, Jackson. We only have ten days to get to Mars."

We got back into the blacked-out ground car, and Jackson directed the driver to take us back. "Keep me updated once you get to Mars. I'll have a pick-up team standing by to take charge of Schecter," he said.

"What's our first move, boss?" asked Goon as the car pulled away.

"We get back to the ship," I said, earning a sour look from Goon.

"For what it's worth," Goon said. "I think we should get Rabbit on that datastick. See what he can find out about Schecter and his business in the Belt. That might lead to some information about where he'll be going once he gets to Mars."

That was exactly what I had planned, but it was good to hear it from our newest partner. I knew Goon was a good operator, handy with weapons and tactically skilled. He clearly was also a smart investigator. He'd been a Federal Provost Agent, so I shouldn't have been surprised.

"Good idea, Goon," I said. Cleo smiled the way she

always did when she caught me being manipulative.

We picked up our own ground car and returned to the ship. Rabbit rolled out onto the catwalk as soon as Sylvia repressurized the hold.

"What's going on?" he demanded. "Where have you been? Jackson was right. I couldn't track you after you got into that ground car and didn't pick you up again until an hour later."

"We met the Colonel," I said. "Jackson has better scramblers than you figured, it seems."

"We have a job?" Rabbit perked up. "What is it?"

"We'll talk in the salon. You have some slicing to do." I held up the datastick, and his eyes lit up. "Also, what's the reward for a war criminal named Tobias Schecter?"

"Three thousand yuan," said Sylvia before Rabbit could look it up.

"He asked me, Sylvia," said Rabbit peevishly.

"But I'm faster," said Sylvia.

I knew better than to get involved when Rabbit and Sylvia were feuding. Instead, I asked, "What's our best time to Tharsis Docks, Sylvia?"

"That depends on how hard you want to push the induction coils and compensators," she replied.

"Can we do it comfortably in ten days?"

"Calculating." Her voice took on that distracted tone she used when she was crunching data. "Twenty-hour 10 G boost, then coast for seven days with an occasional nudge for course correction. Nineteen-hour 10 g deceleration to high orbit. That leaves a little over a day for clearances and landing."

"Lock it in," I said. "Get us a launch clearance and file a flight plan. I want to lift as soon as Rabbit finishes slicing some data."

Goon stowed his weapons in the locker and headed toward his gunsmithing shop and quarters aft of the bulge of the main engine housing. Rabbit took the datastick from me and rolled toward his de facto workstation in the main salon. I hung up the Steinbauer and my knives and secured the locker before following Cleo up the ladder to the second deck.

"Three thousand will barely cover our operating expenses for the month," grumbled Cleo. "We can make more with two charter runs to Highpoint, maybe just one to Alta Hesperion for the right client."

"I know," I said. "But we took the contract and need to show we can do this. Hopefully the contracts will get better. Jackson doesn't trust the Colonel and doesn't want to invest too much political capital in this until it proves out."

Cleo sighed. "I know. And I'm the one who pushed for this. Let's see what Rabbit has found."

I activated my link. "Goon, would you please join us in the salon?"

"On my way, boss," he replied.

We walked into the salon where Rabbit hunched over a virtual keyboard. He must have been routing the data to his link because the holomatrix on the bulkhead across from us was empty.

"Find anything, Rabbit?" I asked as Goon joined us.

He looked up. "Sure, a lot more than just the basics on Jackson's datastick. I broke the encryption on his secondary sources and got into part of the Banker's database, at least the part that deals with Schecter. He goes by the name Sherman now. Theodore Sherman."

He waved a hand, and the matrix filled with a hologram of Shechter/Sherman's current appearance. His round face and pink complexion spoke of his Planitia heritage. He'd had some plastic surgery, and his eyes were now brown and not the blue listed on his dossier, but he still looked like the prison camp guard he'd been under the

Third Directorate. I'd never met the man but knew his reputation as a petty criminal and sexual sadist. The three thousand offered for him seemed low, until I remembered he was assumed to be dead.

"He's still a nasty piece of work," said Rabbit as if reading my thoughts. "He smuggles girls out to the Belt to work in his brothels. Gets them hooked on jolt and pimps them out until they die of disease or lose their looks, then he sells them on to miners as 'domestics,' slaves really. He moves drugs from Mars to the Belt, provides cover for criminals escaping a Martian arrest warrant and relocates them to Highpoint or Ceres. Old man Hong is always hiring."

"So, he's a legitimate bad guy," Goon said. "What have you got that we can use to take him down?"

"I accessed the Banker's schedule." Rabbit moved his hands, and a datebook appeared in the matrix. "Schecter has an appointment ten days from now at 14:00 Martian Standard. I checked the Tharsis Docks database, and Schecter's ship is scheduled to clear customs at 09:00 the same day. Curiously he's also scheduled a cargo delivery, one standard shipping container, a ten by four, at 18:00. Looks like he's drawing cash and buying something for delivery to the Belt. You can fit twenty or so girls into a ten by four if you don't care about sanitation."

"Good job, Rabbit," I said. "Where can we get to him?"

"Docks and the Banker's office are out," said Cleo. "Too crowded. Metternich said he travels with security and even packing sleepers, the three of us can't risk a gunfight in a crowd of civilians."

"We'll need to tail them and look for an opportunity once he leaves the Banker," I agreed. "Maybe when he goes to make whatever deal he's doing. Likely, it won't be out in the open, given his business model."

"Tail will be difficult with just the three of us," Goon

put in. “Especially if he has any counter surveillance backup.”

“If you can get within a few meters, you can tag him and I can follow him through the utilities grid,” said Rabbit. “Then you could hang back and check for other security.”

“How would that work?” I asked.

“Same tracking we used for Deuce back on Highpoint.” Rabbit grinned the smug way he did when he thought he’d been particularly clever. “I’ve modified the Zylene HD delivery system so it’s a two-millimeter gel ball fired from a low power pneumatic. It ruptures on impact and smears a trace of the drive coolant on the target. Mars uses the same leak detection software as Highpoint, so I can follow them on the public utility grid.”

“Won’t Schecter notice he’s been shot?” asked Goon.

“Not unless you hit bare skin. Even light cloth will cushion the impact enough to be unnoticed.”

“Have you got this thing ready?” I asked.

“No,” said Rabbit. “But I can cook up the gel in a few hours and Goon can make the pneumatic in his shop from my design. Shouldn’t take but a couple of days.” He swept his hand across the keyboard that only he could see. “Downloaded the specs to your link, Goon.”

After few seconds spent checking the download, Goon said, “No problem. I’ve got the parts on hand. It’ll take less than two days to fabricate it and retard a pneumatic cylinder to the lower output. Range will be limited, though. Rabbit’s right, a few meters at best.”

“Do it,” I said. “Rabbit, do you need to be on the grid for anything else?”

“No, Zack.” He shook his head and made a folding gesture with his hands. “I’ve gotten all I can from here. I’ve still got the security codes for the Martian systems, so we’ll see what I can find out when we get there.”

"Sylvia?" I called. "Are we clear to launch?"

"Twelfth in the cue, Zack," she said. "Maybe thirty minutes."

"Right, execute the flight plan as soon as we clear the outer marker."

*****

The trip to Mars went off without any problems. We were a legitimate charter vessel after all. Rabbit's gel worked like a charm. Goon tested the pneumatic on me, and even with my nanos, I barely felt the impact. We were as ready as we could be.

Tharsis Docks are chaotic on their best day. We did not land on their best day. Landing clearance took the better part of three hours only to direct us to an occupied pad. We managed to sideslip to an adjacent empty landing pad. It then took another hour to convince the Port Authority we were who we said we were. Eventually, Rabbit sliced a clearance and had a tractor sent out to haul us into the pressure dome. We parked next to a livestock hauler. As long as Sylvia kept the ship buttoned up on our internal life support, the smell didn't penetrate. Any venture outside was a gauntlet of odor and confusion. Livestock was rare on the Moon but was big business on Mars, especially down by Schiaparelli Crater where the Asian descended population preferred fresh to vat grown meat.

Rabbit sliced the Port database and found that we were four hours ahead of Schecter's scheduled arrival. He got a berth number and, assuming the tractors delivered Schecter's ship to the right place, we'd have plenty of time to prepare for an intercept. We drew weapons, Goon taking the Steinbauer pneumatic this time. I took the Czech and Hawley needler. Cleo, as usual, took her stun batons.

We set up outside the docking complex and waited. Schecter wasn't hard to pick out. Better dressed than the usual inhabitants of the docks and surrounded by three burley security guards, he might as well have held a sign above his head saying, "I'm someone important".

Cleo, dressed in a knee length gray dress and head bonnet over her usual combat jumpsuit and carrying a large shoulder bag, looked like one of the Amish colonists who lived out near Olympus Mons. The crowded gates leading to Tharsis City proper forced Schecter's security guards to move in close, less than an arm's length from their primary. Cleo had no trouble getting close enough to tag him on the back of the neck with Rabbit's gel ball. If he felt anything, he passed it off as a random touch from the crowd.

"Tracking," said Rabbit over our links.

"Fall back," I said. "But try to stay within a hundred meters. What direction, Rabbit?"

"Two-hundred-forty degrees relative," he said. "He's headed for Upper Beta."

As the crowds thinned, the security guards assumed a triangle formation around Schecter, one man on point, two flanking behind. We kept them in sight but well back from the flankers. The group reached Upper Beta and approached a busy office block. For the first time, I noticed the cheap aluminum sided briefcase Schechter carried.

The guards stood watch outside as Schecter entered. We watched from across the public passageway that fronted the block. Cleo doffed her disguise, and I wandered through a series of boutique stalls as Goon faded into a shadow near the corner. Schecter emerged about ten minutes later, still carrying the briefcase. The security detail fell in around him and they headed for one of the side passageways that led deeper into the warren.

"He's heading 120 degrees relative and down," said Rabbit. "Looks like he's making for Lower Beta."

"Move up," I said. "We can take him in the tunnels when he gets to the sublevels."

"Let's wait," said Goon. "He's meeting someone. Making a deal or buying something. We can find out who it is and take them both down."

"That's not the contract, Goon," I said. "You're thinking like a cop, not an operator."

"With respect, boss," he replied. "If he's buying people, we need to stop the sale for good, or at least for a while. This job won't pay much as it is, and if we get Schecter as well as his dealer, it'll go further as a 'proof of concept' for Jackson."

I knew he was right, and part of me really wanted to follow his lead. But Schecter was the mission priority, and we couldn't risk losing track of him, despite Rabbit's tracking.

"For now, let's just tail them and look for opportunity," I said.

We followed them into the Lower Beta warren, but instead of a more isolated tunnel, they turned right and approached an open junction. This was an assembly area, a large open square set aside for recreation, public meetings, and voting on election days. From the increasing noise level, there was some sort of rally going on.

The tunnel disgorged into a large open area. Straight across from us a temporary stage spanned most of the far wall. On stage sat twenty children, eighteen girls and two boys. All but one looked to be about twelve or thirteen Standard years old. The oldest boy stood off to one side, looking about seventeen or eighteen. A podium in front of them was vacant but almost as soon as we entered the space, an amplified voice announced,

"Citizens of Tharsis, introducing Ms. Margaret Yoder!"

The announcement was met with enthusiastic applause as a sturdy dark-haired woman crossed the stage to stand behind the podium. She smiled at the several hundred people crammed into the square and made a downward motion with her hands, bidding them to still the applause. It didn't seem to work. Looking around the crowd, I spotted Schecter and his three bodyguards off to one side. He wasn't clapping along with the crowd. Finally, the tumult died down and the woman began to speak, thanking the crowd for their support and kind reception.

"Who the hell is Margaret Yoder," I whispered to Cleo.

"She runs one of the largest war orphan charities on Mars."

Rabbit's voice came through my link. "Margaret Yoder, aged 45 Standard, widow; late husband served as Public Welfare Minister to the pre-Revolution government. She spent the War under house arrest. After Reunification she started Operation Safehouse to shelter war orphans and try to find them adoptive parents. The charity places kids all over the system, from Earth to the Arcologies, even in the Belt."

"So, what's a low life like Schecter doing at a Safehouse rally?" asked Goon.

"Eyes on the target, Goon," I said. "Cover the west exit; Cleo, take the south; I'll stay here and monitor the east."

Margaret Yoder spoke for about five minutes after the crowd settled down. She thanked them for their support and especially their donations. She turned and waved a hand across the seated children.

"These young people are some of the lucky ones," she intoned. "They have been placed with adoptive families from the Archologies to the Moon to the Belt. They will have opportunities for a free and productive life with good families who dearly want a child to love. This is what your help and support have accomplished."

The crowd erupted again, and Yoder waved her thanks

as she walked away from the podium. As a group, the children rose and followed her. The oldest boy and a pair of thick necked men in coveralls flanked and followed them. A few seconds later, so did Schecter and his three security guys. They took the south exit.

"On the move," said Cleo as they passed her. Goon and I joined her, and we followed them. The tunnel twisted to the right and descended. We stayed back, following the sounds of more than twenty people moving in a narrow passageway. The passage opened into a large warehouse space. Yoder stood in front of a ten by four shipping container, watching the older boy close and lock the rear door. She turned to face Schecter.

"Rabbit," I said subvocally. "Can you record this?"

"Everyone, activate your links," he said. "Right, I've got visual from Zach and Cleo, audio from all three of you. What's happening"

"Just record." I extended my nanos, augmenting my hearing.

"You've seen the merchandise." Yoder held up a key fob. "Where's the money?"

Schecter held up a datastick. "On here, as agreed." He extended it and they exchanged the fob and the stick.

Goon stepped into the open, raising his Steinbauer pneumatic and shouted, "Federal agents. Nobody move."

"Damn it," I muttered but moved into the space to flank him.

The guard to Schecter's right drew a weapon, but Goon dropped him with a double tap to the head before he could aim. I shot the point man in the neck with a couple of needles. He got a shot off in my direction that went wide as the drug hit his brain. Schecter tucked in behind the third guard, who had drawn his own Huang pneumatic and managed to train it on Goon.

Goon rushed the man, getting inside his reach before

he could fire. Goon got a grip on the man's gun hand and twisted as he ducked under his arm, pivoted and drove the guard to the ground with a reverse press to his elbow. In another second, the man was flat on his belly, hands flex cuffed behind him with Goon's knee in his back.

Schecter ran for the tunnel, head-on into one of Cleo's stun batons. He went down hard, the aluminum case spinning across the floor.

Yoder turned to run for a hatch just beyond the container, but I was faster. I pressed the needler into her neck. "Not today."

I pushed her to her knees, relieved her of the datastick and zip cuffed her hands behind her back. She slumped to the floor.

The kid who'd locked the container made a break for the hatch but stopped when I shouted, "Hold it right there. I don't want to shoot you."

He raised his hands and turned back to face me.

I waved him over. "Name?"

"Henry," he mumbled.

"Henry, where are the rest of the kids?"

He pointed to the container. "In there. They're all right, there's places to sit, food and water, blankets. They'll be fine."

"Shut up, Henry," Margaret Yoder snarled.

"You shut up," he cried. "You said they'd be adopted. But I ain't stupid. I got a pretty good idea who that guy is and why the *Federales* are here."

"Rabbit," I said through the link as Cleo dragged in an unconscious Schecter and dropped him next to Goon. "Get ahold of Jackson. Tell him we have Schecter, but we need him to send a team from the FBS station here in Tharsis. We'll also need an ambulance and Child Services."

If that last puzzled him, he for once managed to cover it. All he said was, "On it, Zack."

Goon had his man secured and handed the Steinbauer to Cleo. “Cover them for a sec, OK?” He walked over and retrieved Schecter’s case. He brought it back and opened it but found it empty. He frowned and shrugged, closing the case but setting it near his feet.

I rummaged the key fob out of Schecter’s pocket and handed it to Henry. “Open the container. Let the kids know they’re safe and staying here but ask them to stay in there for little while.”

He opened the door and spoke softly and surprisingly kindly to the children. He stepped inside, and I could hear him talking to someone but couldn’t hear what was said, despite my augmented hearing. He came back out and handed me the key fob.

“You’re one of them, aren’t you?” I said.

He nodded. “It was just me and my Da’ before the war. He was killed at Planitia.”

“Why are you helping her?” I pointed to Yoder.

“I like eating and breathing, don’t I?” he said.

I smiled. I liked the kid; he had grit. “Go on, get out of here before the *Federales* show up.”

His eyes opened wide. “*Honto?*” I nodded and he turned and ran for the hatch.

The Feds arrived five minutes later, six men in a combat stack, pulse rifles at their shoulders. They stood down at a signal from their team leader. He walked slowly over to me.

“You’re Mbele?” He held out a hand. “Harris, Team Lead. What the hell’s going on here?”

“Child trafficking,” I said. “It seems Saint Yoder here has been selling kids from her orphan charity to sex merchants like that shithead over there. He calls himself Sherman, but his real name is Tobias Schecter, wanted for war crimes.” I handed over the key fob and the datastick with Schecter’s payment on it. “Evidence. We’re all witnesses and we have audio and vid records of the exchange."

"And the dead guy?" asked Harris.

"He drew down on me after we identified ourselves," said Goon. "It's on the recordings."

Harris grunted and took Goon's name. "There may be an inquest. You'll have to appear."

"Run that by Special Agent Jackson, Lunar HQ," I told him. "This mission is under his watch."

"And the children?" asked Harris.

"In the container. They're not harmed, but we'll need Child Services to take charge of them."

Harris and his team lifted Yoder and the conscious security man to their feet and marched them out. The medics arrived with a couple of stretchers, one for Schecter and one for the guy I'd taken down with sleepers. They covered the dead guard with a body bag.

The Child Services team came in and coaxed the children out of the container. They looked puzzled when several of the kids asked about Henry, but I just shrugged when they asked who that might be. A few minutes and some gentle persuasion later, they had all the kids walking out in a group, just like they'd marched in.

Once we were alone, except for the dead guy, I rounded on Goon. "What the hell did you think you were doing?" I shouted. "I give the orders on this team, not you."

He had the decency to look sorry. "I know, boss," he said. "I should have waited for you to give the word. But I thought Schecter might bolt. And the only way we could get the drop on those guards was if we moved fast. I won't let it happen again."

Cleo nudged the case at his feet. "What's with that?

"I thought he might have some cash in it. Why else would he hang on to it through all this, even try to run with it?" He shrugged. "Maybe I can use it for a toolbox."

A few minutes later, the Morgue team showed up to remove the body. We followed them up the tunnels to Upper Beta and started back to the ship. Goon walked ahead and Cleo and I trailed.

"What do you think?" I asked in a low voice, nodding toward Goon.

She gazed at him thoughtfully. "Well, he did jump the gun, but his instinct about Schecter meeting a buyer was correct. And honestly, Zack, you know you'd have given the order a second later. What other choice did we have?"

"I know," I said. "And if it had been Deuce, I wouldn't mention it. I just don't have a feel for Goon yet."

"It'll take a while." She linked her arm through mine. "Look how long it took you to come around to me."

We got back to the *Profit* a few minutes later. Rabbit sat in his chair, looking down from the catwalk, fairly buzzing with excitement.

"That was great!" He exclaimed. "I got the whole thing on audio from three sources, and the images from Cleo's feed are truly shiny. You should be cleared by the FBS for the shooting, Goon. The other guy clearly drew first." He shook his head. "Margaret Yoder. Who can anyone trust these days? You want me to get Jackson on the comms? The comm lag will be awkward. Maybe we wait until we get back to Tycho?"

"He got the message about Schecter and by now Harris has filled him in on Yoder," I said. "He'll contact us if he needs to. Let's get a launch clearance and go home."

Sylvia got us moved outside the dome with a minimum of hassle. Space inside the pressurized areas was always at a premium. It took a couple of hours to get launch clearance. It wasn't until 22:00 Mars Standard that we were on our way.

Goon sequestered himself in his quarters for much of the trip. He came out for meals and was cordial and even talkative on occasion but seemed a bit withdrawn.

As soon as we cleared the outer marker for Lunar traffic control twelve days later, Jackson called. Cleo and I were already in the salon with Rabbit. I had him put Jackson on the big holomatrix and let Goon know about the call.

"On my way," he replied.

Jackson waited until Goon stepped in before speaking. "Congratulations, *Profit*," he began. "The reward for Schechter has been posted to your account. The evidence Rabbit recorded along with the corroborating key fob and data stick will put Yoder away for a long time. Well done."

"What about expenses?" Cleo asked.

"File a claim," said Jackson. "The forms are in the contract documents."

"Aren't we also entitled to a share of the seized assets?" I demanded. "How much did Schecter have on that money transfer stick?"

"One hundred sixty thousand," said Jackson. "A little low for nineteen children, but that's all there was. Your share will come to about twenty-four thousand, but the payout will have to wait until after Yoder's trial. The money is evidence."

"That could take a couple of years," I protested.

"Read the contract," Jackson said with a shrug. "On the bright side, the higher-ups are very pleased. They've vetted the contract for at least the next two years."

I was pleased with that news but didn't let Jackson see it. I folded my arms with a frown. "Conditional? Not great, but better than nothing. This was your last free ride, Agent Jackson. From now on we want jobs that make it worth our while to risk life and livelihood for the FBS."

Jackson smirked as he reached out to break the connection. "Talk to you later, *Profit*."

I noticed Goon was carrying the case he'd taken from Schecter. "What's with that?"

He grinned and set it on the salon table. "You know I was with the Provost Guard before I joined the FBS, right? Well, part of our duty was Customs inspection. I was actually pretty good at it. You get a feel for who's hiding something after a while. Anyway, the signs were all over Schecter."

"What signs?" asked Cleo.

"The way he gripped the handle of the case and held it close to his body, the way he moved his arm, all suggested it held something he valued. Then, when he had the chance to run, he chose to take the case with him. I was surprised when it turned out to be empty."

"So, why'd you hang on to it?" I asked.

"This is a standard brand-name case, nothing fancy. You can buy one for a few yuan at any discount store in Freetown," Goon said as he hefted it. "And yet something isn't right about it. I realized it was too heavy. One of the things we did in Customs was weigh most of the name-brand suitcases, briefcases, and bags. Caught more than a few folks trying to pass off an empty a bag with a false bottom or hidden compartment." He laid the case flat on its side and flipped up the lid.

"Took me a few days to figure out how to open this thing." A second of fiddling with the corners and he lifted out the false bottom concealing a shallow space beneath the liner. Inside lay two flat bars of shiny metal. "That's two kilos of platinum. At current market value, worth about seventy thousand *yuan*."

"The rest of the payment for the children," said Cleo. "Isn't that evidence?"

"Jackson could have demanded the case if he thought the prosecutor needed it," I pointed out.

"Let's just call it operating capital and see what kind

of price we can get off books," said Goon.

At that, Cleo laughed, and I threw an arm around Goon's shoulder. "Goon, I think you're going to fit in just fine."

Twenty minutes later, I sat alone in the cockpit watching as Sylvia brought the ship into port on a long spiraling flight path. My link chimed. "Mbele here," I said.

"Hello, Zachariah," said Metternich's voice in my ear. "I see you found out about Margaret Yoder."

"Colonel, how are you contacting me? Did Jackson authorize this?"

He chuckled. "I still have some resources that the FBS isn't aware of," he said breezily. "Yoder was the target all along. Schecter was just the vehicle to get you to her. Well done, by the way. A conviction looks virtually certain."

"How did you know about her racket? And why did you care?"

"Again, Zachariah," he said. "I'm not totally without resources. As to why, the reasons are my own. Agent Jackson will be in touch, and we'll talk soon. I think this could be the start of a beautiful partnership." The link went dead, and my heart went cold.

x~x~x

ACKNOWLEDGMENTS:

A novel is a complex beast. Authors work alone much of the time, but we depend on support from a family. Not just the blood kind, but the found kind: editors, beta readers, publishers, and of course, fans. As always, I owe a huge debt to Sharon Skinner for her editorial acumen, her honest criticism and her unwavering belief in my ability as a writer. To Bob Nelson for his good-natured prodding and willingness to push the publish button when presented with a new work, you are a prince, sir. To my wife Michele for her tolerance of my avocation and absences for book fairs and conventions, thank you, my love. And to the fans who willingly spend their beer money to read my books, deepest thanks. I hope never to let you down.

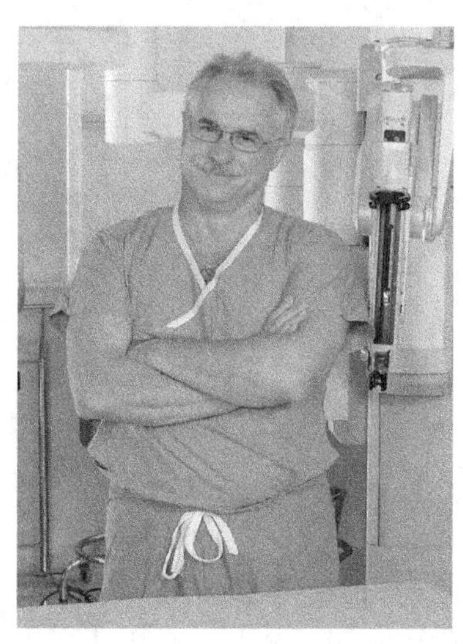

ABOUT THE AUTHOR:

Bruce Davis is a writer of Science Fiction and Fantasy. His current books, published by Brick Cave Media, include the Magic Law series of which Silver Magic is the third installment. It, along with Platinum Magic and Gold Magic are a mash-up of High Fantasy and Police Procedural set in a modern world. Also published by Brick Cave are his Profit Logbook series of SF novels about Zach Mbele, former Martian special forces commando and captain of the fast freighter, the Profit.

In his day job, he is a Trauma and Critical Care surgeon at a Phoenix area Level 1 Trauma Center. His independently published non-fiction memoir Dancing in the Operating Room is a glimpse into the life and training of a Trauma Surgeon.

He lives in Mesa, AZ with his wife who tolerates his passions for writing, science fiction conventions, kayaking, and collecting functional swords and custom knives.